# Drama High, volume 18
## *Rogue*

by
L. Divine

## Praise for *Drama High*

"L. Divine truly made me fall in love with reading."
***Princess Of All*, radio personality from *The Gud Tymez Show***

L. Divine listed as one of the "Great authors for Young Adults".
*-JET Magazine*

"...Attributes the success of Drama High to its fast pace and to the commercial appeal of the
series' strong-willed heroine, Jayd Jackson."
**—*Publisher's Weekly* on the DRAMA HIGH *series***

"Abundant, Juicy drama."
**—*Kirkus Reviews* on DRAMA HIGH: HOLIDAZE**

"The teen drama is center-court Compton, with enough plots and sub-plots to fill a few episodes of any reality show."
**—*Ebony* magazine on DRAMA HIGH: COURTIN' JAYD**

"You'll definitely feel for Jayd Jackson, the bold sixteen-year-old Compton, California, junior at the center of keep-it-real Drama High stories."
**—*Essence* Magazine on DRAMA HIGH: JAYD'S LEGACY**

"Our teens love urban fiction, including L. Divine's Drama High series."
**—*School Library Journal* on the DRAMA HIGH *series***

"This book will have you intrigued, and will keep you turning the pages. L. Divine does it again and keeps you wanting to read more and more."
**—*Written* Magazine on DRAMA HIGH: COURTIN' JAYD**

"Edged with comedy...a provoking street-savvy plot line, Compton native and Drama High author L. Divine writes a fascinating story capturing the voice of young black America."
**—*The Cincinnati Herald* on the DRAMA HIGH *series***

"Young love, non-stop drama and a taste of the supernatural, it is sure to please."
**—*THE RAWSISTAZ REVIEWERS* on DRAMA HIGH: THE FIGHT**

"Through a healthy mix of book smarts, life experiences, and down-to-earth flavor, L. Divine has crafted a well-nuanced coming of age tale for African-American youth."
—*The Atlanta Voice* on **DRAMA HIGH: THE FIGHT**

"If you grew up on a steady diet of saccharine-*Sweet Valley* novels and think there aren't enough books specifically for African American teens, you're in luck."
—*Prince George's Sentinel* on **DRAMA HIGH: THE FIGHT**

Other titles in the **Drama High** Series

THE FIGHT

SECOND CHANCE

JAYD'S LEGACY

FRENEMIES

LADY J

COURTIN' JAYD

HUSTLIN'

KEEP IT MOVIN'

HOLIDAZE

CULTURE CLASH

COLD AS ICE

PUSHIN'

THE MELTDOWN

SO, SO HOOD

STREET SOLDIERS

NO MERCY

SWEET DREAMS


Other titles by L. Divine

THE HONEY SPOT

# ACKNOWLEDGEMENTS

"Life is not easy for any of us. But what of that? We must have perseverance and above all confidence in ourselves. We must believe that we are gifted for something and that this thing must be attained."
-Marie Curie

Thank you to life for knocking me down several times every year, this year being one of the hardest years ever. Thank you to darkness for showing me the opposite of light, and that I don't want to live in the dark. Thank you to light for breaking through all of the hurt and pain and suffering, even in the bleakest of moments. Thank you to joy for always being there, ready to take over as soon as I looked past my own pity party and moved forward. Thank you to faith for believing in me even when I didn't believe in myself. Thank you to hate for never entering my heart even when it would have been justified. Thank you to mercy for teaching me how to forgive during the most difficult of times. Thank you to time for making all wounds bearable, including the ones that have yet to heal. Thank you to love for teaching me that anything is possible as long as I'm willing to work for it. And finally, thank you to my husband, RM Johnson, for choosing us.

# DEDICATION

For the first time in years I rode on a swing today beside my son while watching my daughter catch fire flies in the night sky. I've had a very trying year, and this was the first time that I felt absolutely free on a playground in Hollywood, Florida. This novel is dedicated to the innocence of youth, to childhood before baby daddies and baby mamas, to the absolute freedom to swing and get lost in the melodic groove of the squeak and squawk of a swing set. Get lost, get free, go rogue in your creativity. Only then can you be a blessing to others. This novel I also dedicated to my children for making me laugh, and a special dedication to my daughter, the strongest young adult that I know. To my readers, I promise to up my game and get back to publishing at least two Drama High/Drama U books per year. And last but definitely not least, to all of my mothers for your experience, guidance, wisdom, and divine love. Before and after, there is always family. Always.

## THE CREW

### Jayd
The voice of the series, Jayd Jackson is a sassy seventeen year old high school senior from Compton, California who comes from a long line of Louisiana conjure women. The only girl in her lineage born with brown eyes and a caul, her grandmother appropriately named her "Jayd", which is also the name her grandmother took on in her days as a Voodoo queen in New Orleans. She lived with her grandparents, four uncles and her cousin, Jay and visited her mother on the weekends until her junior year, when she moved in with her mother permanently. Jayd's in all AP classes at South Bay High—a.k.a. Drama High—as well as the president and founder of the African Student Union, an active member of the Drama Club, and she's also on the Speech and Debate team. Jayd has a tense relationship with her father, who she sees occasionally, and has never-ending drama in her life whether at school or at home.

### Mama/Lynn Mae Williams
When Jayd gets in over her head, her grandmother, Mama, a.k.a Queen Jayd, is always there to help. A full-time conjure woman with a long list of both clients and haters, Mama also serves as Jayd's teacher, confidante and protector. With magical green eyes as well as many other tricks up her sleeve, Mama helps Jayd through the seemingly never-ending drama of teenage life.

### Mom/Lynn Marie Williams
This sassy thirty-something year old would never be mistaken for a mother of a teenager. But Jayd's mom is definitely all that. And with her fierce green eyes, she keeps the men guessing. Able to talk to Jayd telepathically, Lynn Marie is always there when Jayd needs her, even when they're miles apart.

### Esmeralda
Mama's nemesis and Jayd's nightmare, this next-door neighbor is anything but friendly. Esmeralda relocated to Compton from Louisiana around the same time that Mama did and has been a thorn in Mama's side ever since. She continuously causes trouble for Mama and Jayd, interfering with Jayd's school life through Misty, Mrs. Bennett and Jeremy's mom. Esmeralda has cold blue eyes with powers of their own, although not nearly as powerful as Mama's.

## Misty

The original phrase "frenemies" was coined for this former best friend of Jayd's. Misty has made it her mission to sabotage Jayd any way she can. Now living with Esmeralda, she has the unique advantage of being an original hater from the neighborhood and at school. As a godchild of Mama's nemesis, Misty's own mystical powers have been growing stronger, causing more problems for Jayd.

## Emilio

Since transferring from Venezuela, Emilio's been on Jayd's last nerve. Now a chosen godson of Esmeralda's and her new spiritual partner, Hector, Emilio has teamed up with Misty and aims to make life very difficult for Jayd.

## Rah

Rah is Jayd's first love from junior high school who has come back into her life when a mutual friend, Nigel, transfers from Rah's high school (Westingle) to South Bay High. He knows everything about Jayd and has always been her spiritual confidante. Rah lives in Los Angeles but, like Jayd, grew up with his grandparents in Compton. He loves Jayd fiercely but has a girlfriend who refuses to go away (Trish) and a baby-mama (Sandy) that has it out for Jayd. Rah's a hustler by necessity and a music producer by talent. He takes care of his younger brother, Kamal and holds the house down while his dad is locked-up in Atlanta and his mother strips at a local club.

## KJ

KJ's the most popular basketball player on campus and also Jayd's ex-boyfriend and Misty's on and off again boyfriend. Ever since he and Jayd broke up because Jayd refused to have sex with him, he's made it his personal mission to annoy her anyway that he can.

## Nellie

One of Jayd's best friends, Nellie is the prissy-princess of the crew. She used to date Chance, even if it's Nigel she's really feeling. Nellie made history at South Bay High by becoming the first Black Homecoming princess ever and has let the crown literally go to her head. Always one foot in and one foot out of Jayd's crew, Nellie's obsession with being part of the mean girl's crew may end her true friendships for good if she's not careful.

## Mickey

Mickey's the gangster girl of Jayd's small crew. She and Nellie are best friends but often at odds with one another, mostly because Nellie secretly wishes she could be more like Mickey. A true hood girl, Mickey loves being from Compton and her on again/off again man, G, is a true gangster, solidifying her love for her hood. She has a daughter, Nickey Shantae, and Jayd's the godmother of this spiritual baby. Mickey's ex-boyfriend, Nigel has taken on the responsibility of being the baby's father even though Mickey was pregnant with Nickey before they hooked up.

## Jeremy

A first for Jayd, Jeremy is her white, half-Jewish on again/off again boyfriend who also happens to be the most popular cat at South Bay High. Rich, tall and extremely handsome, Jeremy's witty personality and good conversation keeps Jayd on her toes and gives Rah a run for his money—literally.

## G/Mickey's Man

Rarely using his birth name, Mickey's original boyfriend is a troublemaker and hot on Mickey's trail. Always in and out of jail, Mickey's man is notorious in their hood for being a cold-hearted gangster and loves to be in control. He also has a thing for Jayd who can't stand to be anywhere near him.

## Nigel

The star-quarterback at South Bay High, Nigel's a friend of Jayd's from junior high school and also Rah's best friend, making Jayd's world even smaller. Nigel's the son of a former NBA player who dumped his ex-girlfriend at Westingle (Tasha) to be with, Mickey. Jayd's caught up in the mix as both of their friends, but her loyalty lies with Nigel because she's known him longer and he's always had her back. He knows a little about her spiritual lineage, but not nearly as much as Rah.

## Chase (a.k.a. Chance)

The rich, white hip-hop kid of the crew, Chase is Jayd's drama homie and Nellie's ex-boyfriend. The fact that he felt for Jayd when she first arrived at South Bay High creates unwarranted tension between Nellie and Jayd. Chase recently discovered he's adopted, and that his birth mother was half-black—a dream come true for Chase. He was also Jayd's first lover and always has her back no matter what.

**Cameron**
The new queen of the rich mean girl crew, this chick has it bad for
Jeremy and will stop at nothing until Jayd's completely out of the
picture. Armed with the money and power to make all of her wishes
come true, mostly via Misty and Esmeralda, Cameron has major plans to
cause Jayd's senior year to be more difficult than need be. But little does
she know that Jayd has a few plans of her own and isn't going away that
easily.

**Keenan**
This young brotha is the epitome of an intelligent, athletic, hardworking
black man. A football player on scholarship at UCLA and Jayd's new
coffee shop buddy, he's quickly winning Jayd over, much to the
disliking of her mother and grandmother. Although she tries to avoid it,
Jayd's attraction to Keenan is growing stronger and he doesn't seem to
mind at all.

**Bryan**
The youngest of Mama's children and Jayd's favorite uncle, Bryan is a
deejay by night and works at the local grocery store during the day.
He's also an acquaintance of both Rah and KJ from playing ball around
the neighborhood. Bryan often gives Jayd helpful advice about her
problems with boys and hating girls. He always has her back, and out of
all of her uncles gives her grandparents the least amount of trouble.

**Jay**
Jay is more like an older brother to Jayd than her cousin. He lives with
Mama and Daddy, but his mother (Mama's youngest daughter, Anne)
left him when he was a baby and never returned. Jay doesn't know his
father and attended Compton High School before receiving his GED this
past school year. He and Jayd often cook together and help Mama
around the house.

# Jayd's Journal

Now that I'm occasionally back riding the bus, I have more time to write in my journal. Good thing, because there's so much going on in my life right now. If I don't keep track of it all by writing it down, I'm liable to forget something important.

Leaving Chase's house and moving back in with Mama has not been an easy adjustment, but it was the right thing to do. The last thing I want is to hurt Chase anymore than I already have. Although he doesn't remember everything, he can tell something's off with me. Honestly, I miss him more than I care to admit.

Esmeralda did her best to harm Chase while she briefly had him under her spell. Thanks to Netta, he wasn't permanently damaged by the encounter. It was hard enough to see Chase caught up because of my battle with the evil wench, but I'll be damned if anyone else that I love gets hurt, again.

Chase was a bit confused about my leaving. I didn't want to go. But with Mama still tripping off being preacher's wife of the year, both her spiritual and hair businesses have fallen on my shoulders. I didn't even go to Inglewood this weekend or work at Simply Wholesome as planned. Time is of the essence, and wasting it under someone else's thumb is not an option.

I haven't heard from Mickey since her and G disappeared with Sin Piedad. I'll check in with Maggie to see if she's heard from her cousins. I would grill Misty for information, if she could recall much of what happened the night I killed her beloved godmother. She does seem to remember slicing my ponytail off with her once-claw like nails. However, everything after that, including me mentally crippling her ass, is a faded memory.

Unlike Misty and Chase, I don't have the luxury of forgetting a thing. It's my job to keep an accurate record of the important events in the life of our lineage. Killing Esmeralda is perhaps one of the most important additions to the spirit book in years. I still can't believe that she's really gone and that I'm the one who got rid of her. Call me paranoid, but I'm not convinced that she's out of our lives for good.

## PROLOGUE

It's been a long week and I'm glad it's Friday. It was extra busy at Netta's shop today, so I will enjoy chilling tonight. I'd rather be in Inglewood at my mom's apartment where I could definitely get some peace and quiet, but I'm too tired to take the long bus ride. Besides, there's always spirit work to do and the back house is the best place to get it done.

As I approach my grandparent's front yard I notice Rah's Acura parked in one of the two driveways. I hope he's not trying to get me to hang out tonight because I'm not going anywhere. Work starts early for me tomorrow, and a sistah needs to get some sleep.

"Hey, girl. Where have you been hiding?" Rah asks, placing his right arm across my shoulders. "And what happened to your hair?"

"I got into a fight with a pair of scissors." I hug my boy tightly and step out of his embrace. We shouldn't get too close physically or otherwise. I'm still sharing a few of my dreams with Rah, and they're only getting more intense.

"Well, I like. It's a good look on you." Rah touches my cropped hair cut, allowing the back of his hand to follow the angle of my left cheekbone. "I never would've pegged you for rocking it short, though."

"There's a lot I'm doing these days that I would've never pegged myself for, either."

Rah doesn't need to know about me losing my virginity to Chase, who can't even share that memory with me, or my killing Esmeralda. The community thinks that she died of a brain aneurism, and that's the way we need to keep it. Maman's sight is not to be messed with, and all of our powers are relatively undetectable by modern medicine, unless you know exactly what you're looking for.

"I want to catch up on what that might be later," Rah says, looking at me like he does in my dreams right before he devours me. "Right now, I wanted to warn you that Nigel's folks have called on the entire LAPD to look for Mickey and Nickey. You haven't heard from her, have you?"

"I haven't seen her since the night Esmeralda died. Mickey and G had Nickey with them when they paid her a visit."

"Why would G go over to Esmeralda's house?" Rah checks his vibrating cell. I know Nigel's worried out of his mind but he has to know that neither of them would do anything to hurt Nickey.

I look over my shoulder and glance at our neighbor's bleak house. "It's a long story. But don't worry. I have my own cavalry out looking for them as well."

"Good shit. I'll let Nigel know." Rah walks toward his car but stops short. "Jayd, what really happened to Esmeralda?" he asks, nodding toward her property.

"She got a taste of her own medicine, and then some," I say, smiling. I can never lie to my oldest and best friend. No matter what kind of drama we go through, me and Rah always come back to the center.

"Bet." Rah opens the car door, starts the ignition, and backs out of the driveway leaving me to contemplate where Mickey might've disappeared off to. I would text Maggie again for an update, but I know she'll get back to me as soon as she knows something.

I pick up a sales paper at the end of the adjacent driveway shared with Esmeralda's property. It's eerie as hell around here now that she's gone. Rousseau and her other animals haven't so much as reared their ugly heads since their master's demise. Maybe I should check it out, just to make sure there aren't any rotting carcasses inside that could become a health hazard. That would normally be a job for Mama, but she's not interested in approaching the dark house.

Only Misty goes in and out of there now. Her mother is still in a coma and it doesn't look like she's coming out anytime soon. I would feel bad for Misty, but she chose her side a long time ago all by her damned self. Ultimately, we all have to live with the repercussions of our decisions no matter how painful they may be.

Lexi creeps out of the open back gate on the other side of the house and runs toward me.

"Hey girl," I say to Mama's German shepherd. Just like her owner, Lexi's gray crown glistens in the setting sun. "Want to be my escort yet again?"

As if she understood all along what needed to be done, Lexi leads the way across the small patch of grass that separates one property from the other. I open the rusted wrought-iron gate and walk up the porch steps. The front door is open, just like we left it the other night. Misty usually goes out of the back door these days.

"Keep your guard up, girl," I say to Lexi who treads suspiciously ahead of me into the dilapidated home.

It looks like a hurricane hit the inside of the house, with furniture turned over, bird seed covering the floor, and dry dog food bags busted open in the kitchen. Dirty dishes are piled high in the sink. The stench is overwhelming.

"We need to get Misty a maid." I cover my nose as I make my way out of the kitchen door toward the porch where, to my surprise, Rousseau is alive and well. Shit.

"Don't worry, girl. I can't harm you," he says without facing me. "Your great-grandmother has made sure of that."

I walk around the beastly man and face him. His once-radiant eyes are dull and cloudy, but his fangs are still as sharp as ever.

"I don't believe that for a minute." Lexi growls at her enemy, ready to attack at my command. "You always find a way to come at me when I least expect it."

"Not this time, ma petite. You've effectively crippled this house." Rousseau waves his right hand around the screened in back porch where I notice the bats, birds, dogs, and other animals are in a seemingly perpetual state of sleep. "I can't even wake them up."

That's not such a bad thing. The last thing we need is Esmeralda's pets running wild around the neighborhood. We have enough strays doing that already without any magical motives for revenge.

"I have my eyes on you, Rousseau," I say, passing him by to walk out through the back yard. I might as well survey the entire property before leaving. A sistah's getting hungry, not to mention all of the homework I have to catch up on. With all that plus work, and Esmeralda's funeral, it's going to be a very busy weekend.

"I would say the same thing, but I can't see a thing." He swats flies away from his face and I can see clearly that he's blind. Maman is no joke.

"Why don't you just leave, Rousseau? Go back to whatever hell Esmeralda dug you up from and leave us alone."

Lexi growls at Rousseau one more time before leading the way home.

"I would, but I didn't bring myself here, little queen," he says after me. "Therefore, I can't send myself away, either. Only your grandmother can do that now. I guess you didn't think of everything when you murdered my beloved, did you?" Rousseau leans back in the patio chair, defeated.

All of the animals awaken and shriek at the mere mention of their former owner. I don't care what Rousseau says, I don't believe for a second that he's completely powerless. I've got to convince Mama to leave Daddy alone long enough to get back on her game. We've got real work to do and she's worried about playing house. There are some things that I don't know yet, and if she isn't going to teach them to me, then I'll have to find another way to get the job done.

*"Crazy is where your power lies."*
*-Netta*
*Drama High, volume 13: The Meltdown*

~ 1 ~

# MIND TRICKS

After a very busy Saturday at work, Mama, Netta, and me came

back to the spirit room to do the final burial rights for Esmeralda's

voodoo doll. Mama arrived late at the shop, leaving me and Netta to do

most of the grunt work, which has been her usual mode of operation

these days. Not only is she acting like a teenager in love, she's let her

hair go wild and curly and started wearing jeans and heels—all at the

request of Daddy.

I hardly recognize the sassier, younger-looking version of my

grandmother. I can't hate her new swag. I just wish her new style didn't

come at the expense of her duties to me, Netta, and our clients. She's

also not trying to hear me about Rousseau, but I have to convince her to

take action sooner rather than later before it's too late.

"I'm telling you, Mama. He's not doing well at all. If we don't do

something soon, the whole house is going to be full of dead animals,

including Rousseau." Talk about a health hazard.

"That's a really disgusting thought, Jayd. Truly repulsive," Netta

says, shoveling the dirt from our makeshift grave onto the side of the large pecan tree. We've got more ritual items buried in this backyard than grass.

"As repulsive as it is, that's about to become our reality unless we do something about it not now, but right now." I take the Florida water from my godmother and sprinkle it into the hole. The sooner we can be done with this burial ceremony, the faster we can get to the urgent matter at hand: cleansing the house next door.

"Jayd, hand me that hammer."

I pass the tool to my grandmother who promptly uses it to put the last nail in the tiny coffin that houses Esmeralda's doll. Without her body, there's not much use for the powerful toy anymore.

"That should do it."

"I'd put another nail through the top, just to make sure," Netta says, passing another one to Mama.

"Netta, one more won't make any difference," Mama says, wiping the sweat from her brow. We've been working nonstop for close to two hours. Burying a priestess is not a task for the faint of heart. "Dead is dead."

"Not when it comes to that heffa." Netta claims the hammer and pierces the center of the wooden box. "Better safe than sorry."

"Agreed." I wink at my godmother before claiming the shovel for the final ritual. "Now, let's bury the witch."

Mama carefully places the coffin into the hole, says a quick prayer while pouring the libation, and then throws a handful of dirt on top. We each take turns sealing the hole and Esmeralda's fate with it.

"Great," Mama says, dusting the soil from her white dress. "I have to meet my honey at Home Depot. We have a date over paint samples."

"Wait a minute," I say, unintentionally grabbing my grandmother's wrist a bit too tightly. Her green eyes shine brightly and I loosen my grip. "What are we going to do about Rousseau?"

"What about him?" Mama says, shaking my hand loose. "He's harmless without Esmeralda's conjuring; always has been." Mama again turns around to walk away but I'm not done.

"So we're just going to leave him there to rot in misery?" I say after her. "That doesn't seem like the right thing to do."

Netta shakes her head in disgust. I know she's feeling the same way I am: totally done with Mama's jaded vision of love.

"Look, Jayd. My husband and I have a lot of time to make up for, and I'm not about to waste another second of it on those people, animals, or whatever else Esmeralda had going in that house. I'm done fighting that fight. We claimed victory once and for all. Isn't that enough?"

"You mean I claimed victory," I say, feeling myself more than I intended. "You were caught up in a Beyoncé video or something, I don't know. But I'm telling you, Mama. Something's wrong over there, and until we handle it properly, this isn't over."

Netta looks from me to Mama, quietly waiting for her best friend's response. For some reason, I'm not afraid of the repercussions my ass certainly has coming.

"Watch yourself, little girl," Mama cutting her eyes at me. "You're sounding more like Lynn Marie every day, isn't she, Netta?"

Netta, not necessarily wanting to disagree with my grandmother from what I can tell, looks sideways at Mama, and continues cleaning.

"Netta, do you have something to say to me?" Mama walks back to our ritual spot and looks Netta dead in the eye.

Netta hesitates for a moment and then speaks up.

"Lynn Mae, you know that I've seen this before. Every time you and your man go through this shit we all have to suffer until y'all are through."

Oh snap. I don't ever remember going through a phase like this with Mama, but I haven't known her as long as Netta has, nor do I ever remember a time when Mama was happy with Daddy. Apparently this is a pattern that I've missed in the cycle of their marriage, but Netta remembers it live and in living color.

"Netta, you can be a spiteful bitch when you want to be, you know that?" Mama says, shaking her index finger in Netta's face.

I think that's my grandmother's version of saying that "haters gonna hate" but I don't want to make any assumptions. Her and Netta have been friends for nearly forty years, so I know that there are some nuisances that I'm bound to miss.

"Spiteful? Me? Really, Lynn Mae?" Netta says, in shock. "Well, ain't that the pot calling the kettle black."

I've never seen Netta and Mama really get into it, but I guess there's a first time for everything.

"Everyone can't have the perfect man, household, and kid like you, Netta," Mama says, practically spitting. "Some people actually have to walk through fire and brimstone and shit to get to their happily ever after." Abruptly, Mama shakes the bottom of her white skirt and heads toward the spirit room, still under Daddy's construction.

"Let this be a lesson to you, Jayd," Netta says, near tears. "Don't fall so far in love that you become blinded by it. Always keep your wits about you, girl. Always."

Netta packs up her things and leaves me alone in the backyard to finish cleaning up the mess we've made. I hope Mama knows what she's doing, and that Daddy knows what she's sacrificing for him, and not for the first time. Maybe I should talk to my grandfather about this. He may be the only one who can snap Mama out of this love spell she's put herself under. It'll have to be tomorrow though, because I am beyond tired, and like Mama said, they've got a date.

*"Jayd, wake up. I know you can hear me,"* the familiar voice says. *I'm asleep but feel suspended between my wake state and a dream.*

*"Let me be,"* I plead, turning over onto my right side and pulling the covers over my head. It's chilly in Mama's room and my blankets aren't much help.

*"I don't have time for your whining, little girl,"* the woman says, impatiently. *"That's the problem with your grandmother. She coddles all of you a bit too much for my taste."*

*"Esmeralda?"* What's this broad doing in my head? I have to be dreaming if she's talking to me again.

*"Of course, my dear. Who else would it be?"*

I can think of several other folks who might visit me before this old shrew, but no such luck. *"Yours is a voice I thought I'd never hear again, and happily so."*

*"That's so sweet, Jayd," she hisses. "I missed you, too."*

*"What do you want, Esmeralda?"* I don't have time to play with her. I need to finish sleeping in order to face the day in a few hours. Unfortunately, I have to attend her funeral today.

*"I wanted to share a secret with you. I've been waiting to tell you this all of your life but your grandmother would never let it happen. Now that I've crossed over as an ancestor she can't stop me from talking to you freely."*

*"When has anyone ever been able to shut you up? Oh, my badd. I guess I did that."* I'm rather proud of my accomplishment, even if I did lose Chase in the process.

*"Or did you?" Esmeralda laughs.*

*"What's that supposed to mean?"* Part of me knew it was too good to be true. This heffa simply won't die.

*"It means that I have no physical form anymore, Jayd. And as such, I'm free. So, thank you. Because of you my physical form no longer binds me. And that leads us back to the original point. The secret."*

"I don't care about your damned secret, Esmeralda. I care about my sleep."

She keeps talking in my head as if I've said nothing. *"I was supposed to be your mom's godmother, and eventually yours. Did you know that?"*

*"You're such a liar. Mama would never trust our lineage to you."*

*"Ask her yourself if you don't want to take my word for it, but truth is truth."*

*"Bye, Felicia."* Dead or not, this broad is delusional.

*"I don't know what that means, but heed my words, little Miss. I don't have to lie to you."*

*"It means you're done talking to me about this and anything else."*

Again, she continues despite my request. *"The book says that the person charged with the spiritual well-being of the child cannot be related by blood. That's why Lynn Marie chose me, her closest god sister at the time of her first daughter's birth, to watch over your mother, the heir to the Queen's Tignon. That's why I moved to Compton. That's why I swore vengeance on your grandmother and her lineage, because she betrayed me. She betrayed my trust by judging the path that I chose rather than honoring her word. Her and her stupid little friend, Netta, decided that they were too good for me, just like a couple of catty witches in high*

27

*school that I easily took care of. But your grandmother's not so easy to get rid of."*

*"You can get out now,"* I say, turning over in bed and tightening my grip on the sheets. This trick is tripping if she thinks I'd ever believe a word out of her mouth, dead or alive.

*"Not until you hear me out, Jayd. You're stronger than your grandmother ever was or ever could be. You, little priestess, have the most powerful and versatile gift of all of your ancestors,"* she says, *physically appearing at my bedside. "The ability to snatch a person's sight in your dreams and wake up with it is not to be toyed with. I can show you how to harness that power and use it in the real world, not hide it like Lynn Mae wants you to do."*

Is she serious? I wish the day would come that I'd choose to work under Esmeralda rather than my own flesh and blood. *"Have you been smoking crack from the grave, Esmeralda? You must be delusional to think that I'd ever leave my lineage to work with you."*

*"Very clever, young one,"* Esmeralda says, her fingernails morphing into claws as she runs them alongside my bedspread. *"My sight isn't all bad, you know. I could teach you how to run your own business through your powers just like I did."*

*"You know what I think,"* I say, sitting up. I need this chick out of my head if I'm going to get anymore sleep before daybreak. *"I think that you're scared I'm going to finally beat you at your own game. My mother left before she was ready, and we all know how that went down."* I momentarily relive the sleepwalking episode where my mom lost her powers to Esmeralda the moment she stepped over Mama's threshold after a horrible fight between Mama and my mom. *"Is this how you tried to lure my mom into your coven? Well, your pimp skills have no affect on me whatsoever, Esmeralda. Now get the hell out of my dream before I throw you out."*

*"Try me, Jayd and you'll see just how afraid of you I'm not."*

Esmeralda disappears just as quickly as she appeared in the first place. What the hell was that about, and how do I keep it from happening again? I'll have to consult with Mama and Netta about the wicked nightmare, and whether or not we need to bury her doll deeper into the earth, or maybe even burn it. There has to be a way to control this shit. The last thing I want is constant pop up visits in my head from the dead witch.

*"There's always going to be drama in life, Jayd. That's just how it is."*
*-Chase*
*Drama High, volume 17: Sweet Dreams*

~ 2 ~

## DEATH BECOMES HER

After last night's dream with Esmeralda, the last thing that I want to do is spend more time thinking about the broad. Her funeral has brought out neighbors from near and far. I think most of the people present just want to make sure that she's indeed dead and I don't blame them.

"Waiting for death to come is very much like waiting for life to appear," my grandfather says from the pulpit. "They each involve unpredictable time, sadness, and relief when the pain ends."

I know Daddy has to be tired of presiding over funerals. It comes with the territory of being a pastor, but still. Having to say nice things about your lifelong family enemy has to be challenging at best. Hell, Mama's not even trying to pretend that she's sad. She's floating around the church like she's on cloud nine.

"There are a lot more people here than I expected," Bryan whispers, chewing on a licorice root.

"That's because they were already here," I say, pinching him on the leg. "At this point it would be rude to walk out. The congregation is obligated to be here until the end of service."

Daddy performs funerals for unsponsored neighbors during the last service, Esmeralda's included. I thought that one of her godchildren would step up and organize her funeral but not a single person did. I think it was more so out of fear than disrespect, but still. That's kind of messed up.

Noticeably absent is Sin Piedad, but Misty, Emilio, and his godfather, Hector, are all in attendance. I'm sure their house will hold it's own special ceremony to bury their matriarch, just as we did for our archenemy.

"Isn't it a glorious day?" Mama says, sitting in between me and Bryan. "Simply beautiful." Mama cools herself with a peacock feather fan, which compliments her bright yellow pantsuit and blue heels. Her outfit is on point, as always.

In a strange way she actually seems in her element here. I think that Mama's loving her reinstated status as first lady of her husband's church. It's a different kind of crown, but still a crown. And she loves rocking her crowns.

"Finally, it's over," Bryan says, rising from the hard wooden pew. "I'm out."

"Hallelujah," Mama says, also standing. "I have to oversee the kitchen duties. I'll see the two of you later."

"Bye Mama, Jayd." Bryan kisses us each on our cheeks and follows the procession into the main hall.

"Later, dude." I watch the two of them head in separate directions and decide that now's as good a time as any to chat with my grandfather.

I wait several moments and allow different members of the congregation to say their goodbyes to Daddy before his duties are over for the time being. I then follow my grandfather downstairs into his office. He takes off his velvet, purple preacher's robe and hangs it on the coat rack next to the door.

"Daddy, can I talk to you for a second?" I ask, closing the door behind me.

"Of course, Tweet. Everything okay?"

"Not really." The recent picture of my grandmother smiling on his desk jars me. As many times as I've been down here I've never see a picture of his wife on display. For the first time, that I can remember, there's also a picture of he and Mama. They look happy and in love, something I never thought I'd say about my grandparents. "Mama's not acting like herself these days."

"Really?' he says, almost snidely. "To me, she's back to being herself for the first time in a long time. As a matter of fact, we're having a sunset picnic this evening." Daddy walks around his desk and sits in the chair behind it. "I don't remember the last time we did something like that."

"I can appreciate that, I guess," I say, walking over to the window and looking outside.

It's a typical sunny day in California, just a little hot for this time of year. I remember playing in the cement lot behind the church as a child during vacation bible school. I didn't spend too much time at church because most of my time was spent with Mama, and she was rarely here when I was growing up.

She served as first lady next to her husband for years before I came along. My birth was what sent Mama back into the spirit room full-time. In a way it's my fault that she and Daddy went their separate ways spiritually, if I think too hard about it. Ultimately, they're both grown and make their own decisions, especially regarding their marriage.

"I'm glad you can, but in all honestly, we don't need you to appreciate it, Tweet." Daddy's stare penetrates me to my core. He hasn't given me that look since he called me an ornery little wench when I was going through my rude phase in middle school. What the hell?

"I know that, Daddy. But I'm concerned that Mama's slacking on her spirit duties and I need her to get back on point. We've got business to handle."

"Jayd, look. I understand you miss working with your grandmother, but I've missed my wife more. And to be honest, our marriage is more important than anything you've got going on in voodoo land."

"Daddy, you don't understand," I begin, but he's not having it this afternoon.

"No, Jayd. You're the one who doesn't understand, and that's because you're young and have never been someone's spouse. God willing, you'll live long enough to get married and have a family of your own one day. Then you'll appreciate what your grandmother and I lost, and found, again with each other."

"But only one of you had to give up your job to get back to that place," I say, not backing down. I've never had to go in with my grandfather, but this is far too serious to give in to their whimsical ideas of romance.

"Your grandmother's job is working with Netta at the beauty shop—always has been. Everything else is a hobby as far as I'm concerned." He leans back and crosses his feet on the corner of his desk.

"Daddy, you know that our work is more than just a hobby. You married a voodoo queen from a long line of voodoo queens. You can't deny that."

"I don't deny anything. Never have. But your grandmother gave up that life to be my wife, and that's all there is to it," he says, proudly. "When she submits to her wifely duties, as the good book says a wife should do, all is right with our world. But, when she goes back into that place that you want her to be in, it throws everything off balance."

My grandfather's always been a traditional kind of dude. He calls it the right and Godly order of things. I call it being a spoiled ass man.

"Mama's a big girl. She can have both worlds in balance at the same time," I say, offended by his rationale. "Why does she have to choose between you and our lineage?"

"I don't know, but I do know that they don't work well together. She took vows, Jayd. We took vows. And we both intend to honor them."

"She took vows to our ancestors, too. Just like you did to the AME church, Daddy. And you can have both worlds. It's not fair that Mama can't."

"Life's not fair, Jayd." My grandfather abruptly places his feet back under his desk, picks up his reading glasses, and sifts through his emails on the desktop computer, effectively dismissing my protest.

"Daddy, I'm serious. We need her." I move closer to his desk and force his attention back to me. "I can't do what needs to be done without her."

For a moment I think I've got him locked into my sight. He breaks our bond and chuckles. He knows our skills.

"Nice try, Jayd. You'll have to find a way to do it on your own because my wife is right where she needs and wants to be," he says, glancing at the picture of Mama on his desk. "I don't mind Lynn Mae doing work for her clients, but Esmeralda's gone, and I'm happy about that. Now we can focus on living the rest of our lives peacefully without the drama next door."

"But that's just it, Daddy," I say, slightly raising my voice. "There's no peace as long as we don't finish the job."

Daddy replaces his glasses on the desk and looks up at me. "I don't know what you're talking about, and I don't want to know. Like I

36

said, your grandmother's happy, Jayd, and alive. Did I mention that? I just presided over the funeral of one of her oldest friends turned enemy. It could've very well been my wife in that casket instead of Esmeralda." He's right. Mama's death is not an event that I want to witness. Just the thought of it brings me to tears. "I personally don't want to bury my wife. But if she keeps it up, she might be next, and I can't stand by and watch that happen."

I get that he's scared of losing Mama. Unfortunately, Daddy's fears can't stop Rousseau. Only Mama can do that.

"Daddy, Mama's never been afraid of losing a battle, and she won't."

"You don't know that, Jayd," Daddy says, lowering his voice to a coarse murmur. "It's not a game we can afford to play at our age. Now, if you will excuse me. I have a date with my wife and still need to tie up some lose ends here. I'll see you later at home." He returns to answering emails.

"We're not done, Daddy."

"Oh, yes we are. And so is Lynn Mae. You're on your own with this one, Tweet." This time he voluntarily locks on to my sight and forces me to feel the full magnitude of his words. It's time for me to go. I know when I've been beat, at least for the moment.

Esmeralda's funeral took up most of my Sunday, but I managed to catch up on my homework and turn it in yesterday. It wasn't my best work, I admit, but it'll suffice for the time being. I have a long way to go until I'm completely caught up with everything, and it's already Tuesday. Without Mama's help, I'm infinitely behind in our spirit work and as long as my grandfather's in control of Mama's will, I don't see a reprieve in sight anytime soon.

"Jayd, what's up, cutie? I love the hair cut," Chase says, hugging me like I'm brand new. "It's like that now?"

"What do you mean?" I pull away and look up at him. God, I miss his lips.

"No, it's not like anything," I lie. "I've just been busy."

"I haven't seen you around since you moved out. I'm kinda missing you, girl. Me and my mom."

"I miss y'all too. It's just that time's flying by and I'm having a hard time keeping up." We walk down the busy hall, barely able to avoid physical contact with the oncoming procession of students.

"I hear that. Can you believe it's already November? Turkey day is right around the corner," Chase says, reminding me of the impending holiday season. "Next thing you know we'll be graduating and out in the real world."

"Don't remind me," I say, eyeing the multiple fliers pinned to the walls of the main hall advertising everything from class rings to prom tickets. "I'm not ready for that yet."

"Please, girl. You were born ready," Chase says. "I have a feeling that you're going to rock whatever college you choose to attend."

I hope he's right. Half of the students from South Bay High will be accepted to the best colleges in the country, and more than ninety-five percent of all students will attend some sort of college. I don't want to be a part of the bottom five percent that end up floating aimlessly after high school if I can help it.

"I don't know about that. I'm so behind in my applications, not to mention registering for the exams." I've got to get my mind right. From boy drama to my girls and grandmother tripping, I've been focused on all of the wrong shit lately.

"Don't be too hard on yourself, Jayd. Besides, you're anything but the average student. I'm sure you'll crush it once you set your mind to it." Chase places his arm around my waist and pulls me in close to him. He has a vast collection of expensive colognes and they all smell good.

Chase has no idea how much I miss him, how much I miss us. If he did, he'd watch the way that he touches me. I'm liable to jump him right here and now if he's not careful.

"Have you heard from Javier and the rest of his crew?" I ask, intentionally diverting my attention away from the memories of me and him making love on the beach, on his balcony, and in his room. He should consider himself lucky for not knowing that we had a relationship. This shit is torture.

"Nah, not yet. I'm sure they'll be in contact soon. Have you asked Maggie again?"

"Nope. Haven't seen her either. Hopefully I'll run into her today. I don't think she was here yesterday."

"I'm sure she wasn't," Chase says. "It's not every day they get to celebrate her becoming the first Latina Homecoming queen at South Bay High. You know her and her family go hard."

"Yeah, they do." I just hope that they didn't go hard on Mickey and her man, G. Maggie's cousins, also know as Sin Piedad or No Mercy, can get ruthless when necessary. I'm worried more about Mickey and her daughter than G, but still. I don't want anyone else going to jail or dying if I can help it.

"Have you heard from your girl?" The way Chase's voice went up slightly in pitch tells me that he's not asking for himself.

"If you mean Mickey, you can tell your boy Nigel that no, I haven't. And for the record, I don't think she's my girl anymore."

"I'm sorry, Jayd. You know that Nigel's got the whole Calvary out looking for her," Chase says, as exasperated with the situation as I am. "Wherever Mickey and G are hiding they're doing a damn good job of it."

"Yeah, they are," I say. "G didn't get this old as a gangster by getting caught."

"True that, Jayd. True that."

"Hi Chase," Alia says, passing us by at the end of the hall. She brushes up against his shoulder like she was forced to do so. It's crowded but not that packed.

"Hey, Alia." Chase turns around and watches her walk away. Her tall stature forces her shapely hips to sway from side to side.

"Really, dude?" I say, not so playfully punching Chase in the gut. "Right in front of me, like that?"

"What's the problem?" he says, feigning hurt. "If I didn't know any better I'd think you were jealous."

Good thing he doesn't know better because I'm not feeling him looking at his ex chick lustfully, or any other broads for that matter.

"I'm just saying. Show a little respect. You feel me?"

Chase's bright eyes probe mine, searching for what I'm not sure, but he's intent on figuring me out. He should know better than to try my own tricks on me. Unlike my grandparents, we haven't been together for decades.

"Okay, Jayd. I don't understand, but I got you. We better get to class," he says, turning down the Math hall. "I'll check you at lunch."

"Okay; cool."

I walk toward the Language hall and take a deep breath. I'm never prepared for Mrs. Bennett's class. Today is not the day to mess with me. I always respect her as the teacher, and as such, her classroom is her territory. But I can't say that she shows me any respect in return, and therein lays our problem. If she stays in her corner then I'll stay in mine.

~ 3 ~

# HOME FRONT

Thank Goddess the rest of the day was uneventful. I made it to work this afternoon without any issues, and we've been busy the entire time. Luckily we're alone and Netta's taking the time to do my hair, which is need of serious repair after its encounter with Misty's claws. My intention was to ask Netta about Esmeralda's claim of being the original candidate as my mom's godmother, but I want to ask Mama first. Besides, I really needed to vent about Chase with someone who knows what happened to him, and to us.

"Unfortunately, joy and pain are two sides of the same coin," Netta says, continuing to drop wisdom on a young sistah. "You can't have one without the other."

Netta's right about that. What would I do without my mothers' guidance? They each have their own unique way of dropping science, and I appreciate it whole-heartedly.

"One of your grandmother's favorite things to say about love is that the more it hurts the deeper the lesson," she continues. "And, more than likely, the harder the love."

Mama can have her love lessons. I'm through dealing with this bull.

"I hate this feeling," I say, fretting my appearance. I don't know who I am anymore, or better yet, I don't recognize myself.

"What feeling is that, Jayd?" Netta bends my head forward, forcing my chin to my chest as she combs my hair from the base of my neck to the front of my head.

"This feeling of being the only one in the know. I mean, there was a relationship with Chase, was there not?"

"Yes, of course there was," Netta says, patiently scratching my scalp. I haven't had dandruff in years, but it sure feels good to have someone working on my head other than me for a change.

"Then why do I feel like it happened in a vacuum? First, I insisted on us keeping it secret. And then, because of Esmeralda's evil ways, the one person I did share it with can't even remember that it ever existed. It's just not right, Netta."

I look at her reflection in the mirror and allow my tears to fall freely.

"Oh, Jayd. I wish I knew what to say to make you feel better but I don't, baby. All I can say is that I'm sorry, and believe it or not, it will get better."

She passes me a tissue and continues to scratch my scalp.

"How will this ever get better? "

"Because, as the good book says, "This, too, shall pass." And when it does, you'll understand why it happened the way that it happened when the time comes. Right now, you just have to go through it. I know that's not very comforting, but it's the truth."

"And I'm expected to go through it all alone, as usual," I whine. "I'm tired of being in love alone."

Netta stops her scratching, puts her hands on either side of my head, and lifts my chin up forcing me to stare in the mirror. "Ah, but you're never alone, child. Never. One thing you must remember is not to get caught up in your own reflection. The mirror can be a tricky thing."

"What do you mean? I'm not narcissistic by any means," I say, thinking of Nellie's selfie addiction before she got caught up in her twisted fairytale with David, that is. It's strange to think that one thing we still have in common is that we both lost our virginity to the same dude, but I'm the only one who knows.

"The mirror is not the only way to see your reflection. Friends, food, material things, thoughts: all of these are reflections of the inner you." Netta resumes combing my hair, but to the back this time. "And when they're taken away, for whatever reason, you can feel less than because you put your self value, your worth as a spiritual being, in those things, and that's always dangerous."

"I never thought about it like that." It's no wonder why so many people my age are lost.

"Yeah, it happens to the best of us. And we, as Oshune's daughters, have the greatest danger of falling prey to false mirrors. Your grandmother is a prime example of that."

Netta walks over to Mama's private station and sifts through several pretty bottles until she finds what she's looking for.

"You think she's caught up in a false reflection, like Esmeralda was in one of my dreams?" I recall the distorted, much younger version of Esmeralda when she tapped into Mama's head. That was a trip. Maybe she was a beauty way, way back in the day. But the Esmeralda I knew and hated was far from it.

"I know that your grandmother's caught up in the version of herself as the perfect housewife and first lady, your grandfather's version of her." Netta parts my hair into five sections where she applies the coconut oil remedy I prepared last week, one of Mama's recipes. "When you find a mate, if you choose to do so, make sure that he appreciates your true self as much as you do. But before he can do that, you have to first be honest about who that person is."

"How will I know who I am if I'm not sure myself?" The scents of lavender and tea tree oil on my temples relax me.

"You'll know when you could give a damn less about what the world around you thinks. The main problem with most women in my generation is that they never took the time to live alone first, or ever," Netta says, massaging the oil further into my scalp. She gives the best deep conditioning treatments. "You really get to know yourself when you're on your own. Jumping from your parent's house to your husband's is not the way to go, in my opinion."

"Didn't you do just that?"

"Yes, Lord!" Netta exclaims, like a church lady. "That's why I'm telling you the truth from both sides, girl. After my son was born, I almost lost every bit of my mind. Not only was I a new bride, but I was also somebody's mama, too. Girl, hell no!" Netta's rubbing becomes more vigorous, but I don't mind. If she keeps going like this I'm liable to fall asleep in her chair. "Don't let anyone ever tell you that the shit's natural or easy. It's a complete shift in identity, and change of any kind is never easy."

"How did you get your mind back right?"

"Luckily I have sisters. That's one thing I know your grandmother always wanted, which is why she kept trying to have more girls. She always wanted women in the house, and I understand that desire. At the end of the day, women are the beginning and end of everything and everyone."

Mama ended up getting six boys in a row instead. But hey, at least she tried.

"Your sisters came and stayed with you? That was nice of them to put their own lives on hold for you." They don't care for my grandmother too much, but they always have Netta's back.

"No, Jayd. They came and stayed with my boys. I left and got a place of my own for a few months. I got my mind back right the only way that I knew how to do it. And my husband understood my need for this. He never demanded that I calm my crazy down. Instead, he embraced the storm with me and let me figure it out on my own."

"Really? You just left your husband and baby to your sisters and lived the single life?"

Netta laughs and shakes her head affirmatively. "Yes, that's exactly what I did. And I have to give credit where credit is due. Every man can't handle their wife leaving for six-plus months while her sisters run his house, but my husband is no ordinary man," she says, wiping her hands clean on the towel over my shoulders. "There's not a day that goes by that I'm not grateful for him. He always encourages me to fly and never tries to clip my wings. That's a real partner for your ass."

"Wow. Does Mama know all of that?"

"Of course she does," Netta says, glancing at Mama's vacant chair. "She was right there all along, helping me cleanse my tiny space and assuage my fears. I was terrified that I was making all the wrong choices, that my husband would find another woman, that I was a bad mother, blah blah blah. But Lynn Mae never judged me."

I'd trade all of my friends and acquaintances for one down-ass person in my life like that.

Netta continues her testimony. "Lynn Mae was just present and did everything I needed without telling me what to do or what she thought that I should do. That's why I'll never desert her, even when she's acting like a complete fool and knows it."

"Why don't you check Mama if you think that she's wrong?"

"Because it's her hell to deal with, not mine. I just wish that she would allow herself that kind of time. That's what the spirit house was all about, originally. It's supposed to be just for her, and you, of course. But it's too close to home to really be a fully independent space," Netta says, sucking her teeth in disgust. "I know what Lynn Marie did wasn't the smartest move, but I do praise your mother for stepping out on her own. She did what your grandmother was always afraid to do. Although she did it all kinds of wrong, she still did the shit, and I admire her fire."

The neighborhood movie and music man knocks on the gate outside, hoping for a sale even though he knows we have no patience for solicitors, just like the sign on the door says. We ignore the intrusion and continue our conversation.

"Yeah, but that was back then. These days my mom's too excited to be a wife, just like every other bridezilla."

"And rightfully so. She's been single for a long time after being married to the wrong man—no offense to your father, Jayd."

"None taken. It's no secret that my mom and dad aren't soul mates."

"Precisely my point. It's her time to do it the way that she wants to, and it's her prerogative to be a bridezilla, as you say. Every woman should be allowed to choose when, where, and how she wants to live in this world. And your mother has every right to make her wedding day as special as she can, even if it is her second time around."

Netta taps me on the shoulder to indicate that it's time for my wash. I follow her to the back and sit down in the chair at the middle sink.

"And Mama? Does she have the right to ignore everything and put her man above it all?"

"Baby, I'm also worried about my friend, but in this case, you need to stay in your place and work on yourself. That's the only person you have any control over, ultimately."

I expected Netta to support me more on that point, but she's got Mama's back to the end. "If you say so."

Netta hands me a mirror and runs her fingers through my crudely cut tresses. "Let's do something different, Jayd. Trust me. A new hair style will make you feel better."

I doubt it. Between Mama tripping and Chase forgetting all about us, I'm feeling worse than usual. "I think it's going to take a whole lot more than a new hairdo to get me out of this funk."

"It all starts with how you see yourself, little girl. You better than anyone should know that by now."

Netta points at my reflection. Initially, all I can see is the jacked up haircut Misty left me with, and the dark circles underneath my eyes from a lack of peaceful sleep. After a few moments of Netta in my head again, I start to see the new me beginning to form.

"I say we go for it," she says, pulling my hair into shape. "Let's do a few highlights all over, brighten you up a bit. It'll compliment your features real nice. We'll braid it, set you under the drier, let the braids out, and let your natural curls fall where they may."

Netta has a real knack for making her clients look better than they could've ever imagined, including me.

"Untamed. I like it!"

"So do I, little queen. So do I."


I can't wait to show Mama my new hairdo. I don't know if she'll be happy about the cut and color, but I love it.

"Mama, are you back here?" I call before opening the door to the spirit room. It would be nice to walk in and see her back in the habit of mixing ingredients and feeding our ancestors, but no such luck. Instead, it looks like I've interrupted an evening quickie.

"Jayd, I thought you were spending the night at your mother's apartment tonight?" Mama says, rising from the mat on the floor in the main room.

Daddy doesn't even bother to get up. He looks content to stay right where he is, damn the intrusion.

"I am, but I thought I'd check on you first and show you Netta's handiwork." I step into the kitchen and meet her half way.

"It looks lovely, dear. You better get going before it gets dark. The last thing you want is to ride the bus all the way to Inglewood late in the evening."

She doesn't have to ask me twice; I can take a hint.

"Bye Daddy, Mama." I close the door behind me and hear Mama latch the chain at the top. I've never been completely locked out of the spirit room before. Mama has really lost her mind for that one, but it's ultimately her house and there's nothing much I can do about it.

"I guess it's just you and me, girl," I say to Lexi, who's also been uncharacteristically locked out of the back house she's usually charged with protecting. Everything changes when a man moves in, and not always in a good way.

Suddenly a strange sound comes from next door. The howl gives me shivers. It doesn't sound human or other, but both. I look down at Lexi who growls a low, guttural sound. I can tell that she's more afraid than brave.

I peek over the fence and see Misty walk out of the back door and onto the cluttered porch where I last saw Rousseau, who's noticeably absent. She bends down and feeds all of the animals in cages and on leashes. When she reopens the back door a large black bat flies out and lands on one of the beams on the ceiling. It hangs upside down and accepts food directly from Misty's hand. Something's not right about the flying rodent. I've seen it before but can't place exactly where. Not to say that there couldn't be animals over there that I've never seen before, but that bat is familiar to me.

Damn it. I know I'm going to have to go back inside of that house and soon. It's the last thing I want to do, but I don't have much of a choice. Apparently I'm the only who's willing to do what's necessary for our protection. The work has to be done, and I'm going to need the help of our ancestors to do it. I'll say a special prayer tonight at the altars in Mama's bedroom to help us through, since I no longer have full access to the spirit room. I'll also pray for patience, because Mama's testing all of mine lately.

*The stench of animal smells, including shit, is overwhelming. I hold my breath and walk further into the barn where Esmeralda's brood is sedated in a trance-like state. Perfect. This will make my job that much easier. I hate to sacrifice all of the innocent animals, but as long as they're alive they're also susceptible to Esmeralda's trickery, even from beyond the grave.*

*"Not so fast, Jayd," Misty says, emerging from behind one of the many tall stacks of hay lining the walls. "I don't think my godmother would appreciate you killing off her progeny."*

*"I don't give a damn what she appreciates. They need to go, and*

*you can either watch me do it or leave."*

*"And just how do you plan on getting past me?" Misty walks toward me slowly, never dropping her eyes locked in on mine. "I'm not a little girl anymore either, Jayd. Like you, I was forced to grow up too soon."*

*Misty's steady strut becomes a jog until she's running full speed ahead. Before she reaches me, she stretches her arms out and takes flight, changing shape into a gray owl. What the hell?*

*I swing at the large bird with all my strength but it's no use. She continues her attack, poking holes in my forearms and forcing me to retreat outside, defeated.*

*"You must go back in and fight, I don't care if it hurts!" Maman screams into my thoughts.*

*I nurse my bloody wounds and catch my breath. That's easy for her to say. She doesn't have to fight off the scary looking, rodent eating, and big ass bird trying to kill her.*

*"Maman, I can't defeat an owl. That bird is no joke." My arms hurt and so does my head, much like when Esmeralda stared at her victims. "I'll have to find another way to get rid of them."*

*"This is the only way, little girl. Get your ass back in there and finish the job. They're just animals, including the damn owl. You control them, not the other way around."*

*"I thought Esmeralda controlled them?" My head pounds hard, making it nearly impossible to focus on the task at hand. I've never experienced a migraine, but I think this is as close to one as I've ever been.*

*"Yes, she does. And she also left her psychic footprint in your mind, did she not?"*

*The pain turns into a loud pounding. Suddenly my sight is redirected toward the closed door. It still hurts, but the pain feels more like power than weakness.*

*"I guess she did."*

*"Whether she realizes that she left her residue behind or not, consider it a gift from her invasion. Use what she gave you to control her creatures and get the job done."*

*"I can't do it, Maman."*

*"Look, Jayd," My great-grandmother says, petulantly. "We don't have time for self-doubt. I know this feels like the opposite of everything that your grandmother has trained you to do, but trust me when I say that sometimes you have to walk a thin line between two worlds." Maman sounds more like Esmeralda than Mama. "There's not always a right or wrong way to do things, but there's only one right answer. We all know how to choose better, or worse, and a select few of us can choose to exist*

*somewhere in between. This is one of those in between times. Now, stop*

*pussyfooting and get to work."*

*With my newfound vision I push the red doors open and locate my*

*first victim perched on a rafter. The oversized owl swoops down and heads*

*for my head. I lock onto her beady black eyes and stop her mid-flight.*

*Back to her human form, Misty falls to the ground and writhes in pain. I*

*don't miss that feeling at all.*

*"Sorry, y'all." I lock onto each animal one by one, using their*

*owner's sight against them until the very last one is permanently disabled.*

*Esmeralda walks in behind me and screams at the top of her lungs.*

*"All the shrieking in the world won't bring them back," I say,*

*unemotionally.*

*Misty moans in pain as she sits up. She looks sorrowfully at her*

*godmother who joins her on the ground. My job is done, for the moment. It*

*wasn't pleasant and I didn't want to do it, but it had to be done.*

*"Welcome to a queen's world, mon amour." Maman Marie leaves*

*my head, and I leave the two of them alone to mourn their loss.*

*"You shouldn't throw around words like that haphazardly, Sandy. They may get you into more trouble than you bargained for."*
*-Jayd*
*Drama High, volume 12: Pushin'*

~4~
# THE WITCH, THE PSYCHIC, AND THE VOODOO PRIESTESS

After my run-in with Mama and Daddy yesterday evening I've been feeling really strange, and not just because I interrupted their booty call. Last night's dream about Misty didn't help much, either. Whatever she was doing over there yesterday with Esmeralda's pets crept into my subconscious and scared the hell out of me. Something's not right and I have to find out what's up with her, whether I want to or not.

"Jayd. Look at you, girl. I hardly recognize you," Ms. Toni says, stopping me in the middle of the main hall. It's been too long since I had a heart-to-heart with my school mama.

I reach up and hug her tall, thin frame. "Sometimes I hardly recognize myself."

"Ha! I know that feeling." Ms. Toni steps back and gives me a good once-over. "Seriously, Jayd. You're looking more like a grown woman every day. What happened to the loud yet reserved sophomore who first stepped into my office three years ago?"

"She kept living," I laugh. I remember that day like it was yesterday. I was so frustrated with my new school environment and went to the only black teacher to vent. And she welcomed me with open arms.

Ms. Toni smiles as her eyes tear up. "Indeed she did, and I'm so proud of her."

"How have you been?" I ask, as we continue walking down the near-empty space.

By the time the last class period arrives, half of the seniors have left campus early, which thins out the traffic in this hall where the majority of junior and senior lockers are housed. I truly hope that I can work out my schedule to leave after lunch next semester. The less time I spend at this school, a.k.a. Drama High, the better.

"I've been good, girl. No complaints. How about you, other than the new hair?"

Lying to Ms. Toni has never been possible. She can always tell when something's up.

"Actually, life has been really challenging lately."

"Oh, you're going to have to be much more specific than that, Miss Lady."

We stop in the middle of the hall in front of the Associated Student

Body door where her office is housed. I wish I could hang out and chat, but I have a study session in the library in a few minutes.

"Let's just say that I need a new crew to hang with, and soon."

"What's new?" she says, with one hand on her hip. She has enough sass for every black woman in the South Bay Area, in case any of them are lacking. "Let me tell you something, child. Life's always going to be a challenge, remember that. It's how you face that challenge that determines whether or not you're living life to your fullest capability. And if the people that you surround yourself with are more of a hindrance than a help drop them quickly, and don't look back or you'll end up like Lot's wife."

"Lot's wife? That sounds biblical."

"Indeed. It's one of my favorite bible stories. The basic lesson is that when you know you should keep moving forward and you look back, don't be surprised if you turn into a pillar of salt."

"Sounds reasonable," I say, sarcastically. "But I feel you. No reminiscing over the past."

"Pretty much. If God takes something or someone out of your life, leave them out, even if it's the hardest decision you've ever made. You never know what She has in store for you, or what hell She may have just saved you from."

I love how Ms. Toni refers to God as a She. Sometimes she'll say He as well, but it's always a balanced reference.

"Want to come inside? I added some new books to my collection that I've been waiting to share with you." She opens the door where Reid, Laura, and the rest of the ASB members are inside meeting about one event or another.

"Can I take a rain check? I have to meet some of my classmates in the library for a study session."

"Of course, Jayd. I'm here anytime."

"Thank you. Have good afternoon."

Ms. Toni gives me another hug. "You too, baby. And remember, don't look back, no matter how tempting it may be." She steps inside and closes the door behind her.

When I turn around to head toward my locker, Misty walks through the side entrance. She looks completely dazed and confused, much like she did once I was done with her and her animal siblings in my dream last night.

"Misty, are you okay?" I ask, passing her by. Not that I should care about her well-being, but she's looking unusually tossed this afternoon.

Misty abruptly stops her trek and shakes her head. She looks around the main hall like she's shocked to be here. Was she sleepwalking or what? I've been there so I know how confused she can feel, if that's truly her issue. It's the end of the day, so I don't think that's the case. But anything's possible in our worlds.

"Yes. Why wouldn't' I be?" Misty says, combatively.

"Forget I asked."

Misty rolls her eyes at me, gives a not-so-nice gesture, and walks away. The trick will get everything she deserves and more by the time I'm finished with her household.


When I finally make it to the library, Alia and Marcia are nowhere to be found. I guess they're running late, which is fine with me. I need a moment to collect myself anyway. It's been too long since I actually gave my full effort in a study session. That's going to change starting today. If I don't get serious about the SAT and my college applications, I'll be left behind and that's not cute at all.

"Jayd, my favorite lady," Jeremy says, catching me off guard.

Until his drug possession case clears he's on lockdown either in the office or the library. It really sucks for him because he also lost his driving privileges again and subsequently has to wait for one of his parents or brothers to pick him up. He can't even call Uber or a car service because he has to be released into the custody of an adult family member. Cameron really did a number on him. If he had more of a backbone he wouldn't be in this predicament in the first place.

"What's up with you, Jeremy?" I say, giving him a quick hug.

He tries to linger a bit too long and I back up. I'm taking Ms. Toni's advice on several different levels. The last thing we need to do is go backwards.

"Nothing much. Just playing a game of solitary chess before my brother gets here. He's always late."

"I hate waiting on folks. I can't wait to get my mom's car fixed, or rather get the money to get it fixed."

"And I can't wait to get my freedom back." He doesn't have to remind me that I'm supposed to be making something extra special to help his court case. A sistah's just overly busy these days, but I'll get around to it, and he knows that it goes without saying. I always keep my word, even when I probably shouldn't.

"I hear that. Well, I'm here to meet my study group, so let me find a table for us. Hope your brother gets here soon."

"Wait, girl. What's the rush?" Jeremy asks, stopping me with his smooth tone. How I do miss our late night conversations over the phone, and in person. "You have time for a quick game, don't you? For old time's sake?"

I look into his once-mesmerizing blue eyes and smile. "No, I don't. But thanks for the offer."

"Come on, Jayd," Jeremy pleads. His ways are still so enticing but unfortunately for him I'm no longer under his love hex. "I haven't had a good challenge in a long time, since the last time we played, actually."

I must admit that I do miss a lot of things about our relationship, including our intellectual flirting. And Cameron doesn't look much like the chess type. She prefers games of a more sinister nature.

"Fine, I can beat you real quick. It'll help me focus on the testing material." I place my backpack and purse in one of the three empty chairs at his table and take a seat in the one directly across from my opponent. Every time I get too close to Jeremy I remember everything I used to love about him. Too bad the respect is gone. Without it, no relationship will prosper no matter how much love there may be.

"Excellent." He sets the board. "Black or white, my lady?"

"Black."

Jeremy smirks. "I see your strategy hasn't changed much since the last time we played."

Jeremy moves one of his two knights out front.

"Neither has yours." I contemplate my next move. I only know of two ways to win from this vantage point. And I only need three moves to do it.

"Why do you insist on moving your pawns first?" Jeremy asks, moving the pawn closest to the exposed knight up two spaces. That's his second mistake so far.

I move the bishop that my pawn just freed diagonally across the board. "Because they're the most underestimated pieces on the board."

Jeremy considers his options and his adversary carefully before doing as I expected. "What do you know about this right here, son?" Jeremy says in his best New York accent. I can't help but laugh at his confidence, even if it's misplaced. "You know I've got you in check within the next move or two, right?"

"You see, that's the problem with being cocky, my friend," I say, moving my bishop closer to his side of the board. "There's always someone waiting in the wings to knock you off your pedestal."

Jeremy eyes the board, thinking three steps ahead, if I know him as well as I think that I do, and shakes his head. "Really, young master? How is it that you're so good at teaching others how to defend themselves in chess and life, but you rarely do the same for yourself?" He frees his other knight, effectively trapping my bishop and thwarting my plan.

"Shit."

"Never let your enemies see you sweat, Jayd. Never."

"I wasn't aware that you were my enemy." I consider my options and decide to free my queen.

"You're showing your hand a bit early, aren't you, Lady J?"

"It's never too early to win, and she always gets the job done. Always."

Jeremy makes his next move. "Just like someone else I know. Doesn't surprise me that you would take that kind of risk. You've always been a rogue of sorts."

"What's that supposed to mean?" I ask, trying to figure out his next move, both on the board and with me. He knows how to pique my curiosity, that's for sure. It's almost the same thing Maman Marie said in my dream last night.

"It means that you know better, and you know worse, but choose to exist somewhere in-between, just like the queen of the castle. She can move any way she needs to in order to handle business, even if it's right into the line of fire.

Jeremy eats my queen and traps my king. "Check and mate."

Damn, I didn't see that coming. "Well, I guess that's game." I reclaim my things and stand.

"Wait, Jayd." Jeremy also gets out of his chair and takes my hand.

"What is it, Jeremy? I gave you your game, you took me to school, now I need to get my study on." I smile at my ex and squeeze his hand. "No hard feelings. I needed the refresher."

"I enjoyed it, too, but not because I won. I've been playing chess in here to keep myself from going crazy. The thing is that I love you. And even more that, I miss you. I miss us." Jeremy bends across the table and moves in close to me. He touches his nose to mine. Damn, he smells good.

Thankfully Marcia and Alia walk into the building right on time.

"Are we interrupting?' Alia asks, all smiles.

Marcia blushes at the obvious intrusion. I know that she's still feeling my ex boyfriend just like I'm feeling Alia's.

"Not at all. I was just about to get us a table near the back windows."

"We'll meet you over there." Alia tugs Marcia's jacket. "Bye, Jeremy."

"I'll see you later," I say. "And don't worry. I'm still working on your case."

"I know you are, Lady J. If anyone can fix this mess, it's you."

"Thanks for the game." I try to walk away again but Jeremy's not done quite yet.

Jeremy tightens his grip and forces me to look at him one more time. "I need you in my life, Jayd. However we can make that work. I know you've got my back just like I hope you know that I've got yours."

He finally releases my hand, and I join the girls at a table by the restrooms. Perfect. I can go inside one of the stalls and cry for a moment before getting to work. I'm so tired of being emotional over dudes but it seems to be a permanent part of the territory. Hopefully one day I'll learn to deal with it better than I am today.

After about an hour of creating flashcards and reviewing testing materials we're more than ready for a break. The studying has been a welcomed distraction from thinking about both Jeremy and Chase, but it's not a miracle worker. I miss them both, but one much more than the other. I feel sympathy toward Jeremy instead of the passion I feel for Chase. I hate to say it, but I think I've lost respect for Jeremy as well. He's not a coward in all ways, but he's got cowardly tendencies, and that's not attractive.

"I brought some snacks and bottled water," Alia says, pulling out the contraband items from her *Trader Joe's* shopping bags. "The cookie wrappers are quiet so we shouldn't disturbed anyone, especially the librarian."

The three of us look across the room at Mrs. Hawk before opening the packages. She's notoriously strict with her house rules.

"Look what I brought with," Marcia says, like she's smuggling cocaine. She sets the aged cloth-covered pile down on the wooden table and unwraps it.

"What is it?" Alia asks, curiously.

I'm too tired to feign excitement. My brief encounter with Jeremy took what little reserved energy I had left to deal with the rest of the day, and it's far from over.

"It's a Tarot deck that my mom gave me on my thirteenth birthday. She said it was the year of enlightenment, and she was right." Marcia expertly shuffles the pretty circular cards. I'm impressed.

"I don't know if we should play with those here," Alia says, looking over her shoulder.

"What's the big deal? It's just a deck of cards," I say touching the deck. "I love the female centered drawings. How old are these?"

"I don't really know," Marcia says, continuing her shuffling. "My mom got them from her mom, also on her thirteenth birthday, and I know that my grandmother had them before that."

"Nice." I like that Marcia's maternal lineage has similar traditions to my family ancestry. There's always been something eerily familiar about her, and it's not just her bright eyes.

"Seriously, we shouldn't play with these types of things," Alia says, concerned. "My psyche is very sensitive. I played with a Ouija board once and it took me months to stop having nightmares."

At least hers stopped. My nightmares, like my dreams, are an ever-present part of my daily life.

"Alia, this isn't the same thing," Marcia says, spreading the deck Alia's way. "Pull a card from the top of the deck and we'll read its energy."

"No thank you. I'm all for a study break but not like this."

"You're missing out, Marcia says, reshuffling the deck. "Jayd, will you play?" Marcia places the deck in front of me. "It's fun."

"Why not." I split the deck in half like I'm playing Spades or any other card game with my Uncle Bryan, and pull a card from the top.

"The Fool. Very interesting," Marcia says, opening the well-read booklet accompanying the deck.

"See. I told you this game is stupid." Alia scoots her chair back up to the table.

"Is your deck seriously calling me a fool? Thanks." I laugh and shake my head from side to side. Even the damned cards have it out for me.

"No, Jayd." Marcia shows me the page with the card's description. "This is one of the best cards to be dealt. It's the Alpha and Omega of the major arcana."

"What does that mean?" Alia says, now looking at the deck inquisitively.

I stare at the happy dude dressed in a court jester's costume looking up at the sky. "He looks like he's going somewhere." I touch the red bag tied to the end of the stick slung over his shoulder. He kinda reminds me of Papa Legba, my father orisha.

"Yeah, over that cliff," Alia says, pointing at his feet. It figures that I'd pull a card where the subject's stepping into danger. That's all I seem to do lately.

"True, metaphorically speaking," Marcia says, pointing at the card. "The mountains in the background represent adventure, and the cliff is stepping out into the unknown in order to discover your true self beyond your worst fears."

Sounds like what Netta was talking about the other day. It's also reminiscent of Esmeralda's suggestion in our last dream. Maybe Marcia's cards are on to something.

"That's not so bad," Alia says, adjusting her view. I bet she wishes that she had pulled the first card after all.

"You're on a journey of self-discovery, basically. The universe is telling you to enjoy it and don't be afraid." Marcia points at his red satchel. "You have more knowledge in your bag of tricks than you know."

A slow chill moves from the top of my head to the center of my chest. There's so much truth in Marcia's words that I can't even speak. The girl's got mad skills reading the cards.

"What's up with the dog?" Alia asks, noticing the pooch at the Fool's feet. "And the sun?" Alia's unfounded fears seem to fade as her curiosity takes over.

"The dog represents protection on the path, and the sun is a symbol of enlightenment. It's truly a beautiful card, Jayd." I never thought a fool could be deemed as beautiful. "Sometimes it's good to be foolish when embarking on a new path."

"I don't know what to say." I'm truly stunned. "Thank you."

"Don't thank me. I didn't pull the card, you did. I just call them like I see them." Marcia replaces the card into the stack and reshuffles the deck. "Have you ever had a reading before, Jayd?"

"No." At least not like this. Mama reads the cowrie shells when necessary, but we haven't done that since my last ceremony months ago.

"Neither have I." Alia's eager for her turn, but Marcia keeps shuffling. "Can we ask it questions?"

"Yes, but I prefer to take my chances at random. My grandmother's good with reading full spreads that give your life's story.

There are so many ways to read the cards. She even throws the iChing, an ancient Chinese method of divining."

"Can you do that?" Alia asks. "I've also heard of voodoo priestesses giving readings about your life, kinda like a fortune teller."

"Voodoo priestesses are not fortune tellers. Those are gypsies." I can't help but to correct when a person groups all of the powerful spiritual paths into one stereotype, usually when it refers to women practitioners. Every system deserves it's own recognition.

"Jayd, people believe in such things as witches, psychics, and voodoo priestesses, believe it or not." Alia thinks she's saying something brand new, but she's not. But now isn't the time to discuss her white privilege. "Do you know that there's this dead woman in New Orleans that people still pimp out for profit?" Sounds like a little of Chase's black may have rubbed off on Alia while they were dating. "Mary Larue or something like that. I went to her tomb last summer with my parents. Very eerie shit."

"You mean Marie Laveau," Marcia says, matter-of-factly. If I didn't know better, I'd think it was her great-grandmother's name being slaughtered instead of mine.

"Oh yeah," Alia says. "She was in American Horror Story: Coven a couple of seasons ago."

Marcia becomes visibly irritated with every word that comes from Alia's mouth. "No, she wasn't. Angela Bassett was. Marie Laveau isn't an actress. She's the real thing; a real voodoo queen."

Damn, Marcia's very protective of Maman. What does she know about her?

"Why so serious, Marcia? It's not like she was a real person either way," Alia says, flippantly. "She's just myth to sell tours in NOLA. Her body's not even inside the tomb."

"No, it's not," I say, feeling Maman's sight overpower my own. Oh, hell. I don't want to go off on Alia, but we've all had enough of her advantaged innocence for one day. "That's because a priestess cannot simply be buried in some concrete slab for people to gawk at," I say, looking at Marcia. "She returns to her true state, to nature itself. But veneration is lovely, indeed."

Marcia's excited about my knowledgeable backup. "Exactly. A true witch doesn't allow her energy to be misused, even after her death."

"She was never alive!" Alia says, impatiently waving her hands above her head. "You two really need to stop watching so much television."

If she only knew how little of it I watch on a regular basis. The spirit book is more of a reality show than anything streaming live or otherwise.

"And you need to open your mind," Marcia says, covering the cards with the purple cloth and replacing them in the side pocket of her backpack.

"Not to fables I don't." Alia refuses to accept that Maman could be a real person, and that's just fine with me. Mystery and suspense serve our lineage well, and doubt only strengthens our resolve. As long as our clients have faith in our history and that's all that really matters.

Chase walks into the library and heads our way.

"Ladies," Chase says, bowing like the prince charming that he is.

We each smile. I love my silly friend.

"We're wrapping up our study session now," Alia says, placing her heavy textbooks inside of her bag. "You should join us next time."

"Nah, I'm good. Besides, I'm banking everything on my personal essay and how I'm the anti-Rachel Dolezal, hair and all." Chase removes his baseball cap and points at his clean-shaven head.

"Seriously?" Marcia asks, looking up at Chase with a smirk on her face.

"Yeah, girl. Colleges are saps for the poor, adopted, sob story. And then, when I add my racial flavor to the mix, I'm as good as in. Trust, my shit's going to be unstoppable."

Only Chase would think that he could hitch his entire college career on three pages. I'm sure his family's ability to pay tuition at any institution he chooses without financial aid helps his application as well.

"Studying couldn't hurt, even with all of that genius on the page," I say, closing my books. I agree with Alia on this one. Besides, it would be nice to see him afterschool on the regular. I'd have an excuse to be around him.

"We can always hold private sessions if you don't want to be here." Alia stands up and hands him her bag. What did I miss?

"Sounds like a plan," Chase says, kissing Alia. What the hell? His phone rings inside of his back pocket and stops their public display of affection. "I have to take this. Meet you outside, baby. Ladies."

"Are you two back together?" Marcia asks, taking the words right out of my mouth.

"Yes," Alia says, enthusiastically. "I'm glad me and Chase found our way back to each other. He's my soul mate. I just know it."

"There's no such thing," I say. I'm more than salty with this new development. I'm downright pissed, and yes, slightly jealous of her ability to freely love the man that I love. "If it were true, I wouldn't be alone and neither would you, right, Marcia?"

"Speak for yourself," Marcia says, collecting her things. "I have a man back in San Diego, which is why I was sent to this hell hole. We speak every day. Even with the distance, he's still in love with me and I with him."

"Yeah, okay." It's time for me to leave before my bitterness takes completely over. I'm so done with girls surrendering their good common sense to be in love with dudes.

Alia and Marcia look at each other, shocked, and then back at me.

"Jayd, I feel for you. I used to think that you were so strong and bold," Alia says, looking past me toward the front door where Chase stands outside. "Now I see that you just need somebody to love you the way we all deserve to be loved."

"Alia, please. Trust that I'm good in that department."

"As long as you're not giving yourself away in the process, love is a great thing." Marcia sounds like she's deeply sprung.

"Agreed," Alia says, walking toward the entrance. "See you two tomorrow."

"I'm out, too. Later, Jayd." Marcia follows Alia out, and I notice that Jeremy's finally gone, too.

Marcia's right. No more giving away my ashe to dudes. I'm also done providing my services for free. If Mama doesn't want to get paid, I surely will do it and happily so. Shit, I think I'm going to charge Jeremy and Mickey for their work this time around. Why should I be the only one not taking advantage of all my talents? Just like my clients—friends and frenemies included—I have to get my hustle on and leave love alone for the time being. My hustle just so happens to help other hustles, too.

*"When is enough ever enough?"*
*-Misty,*
*Drama High, volume 17: Sweet Dreams*

~5~
# WHO RUNS THE WORLD?

One of the prescriptions that Netta gave me after having my hair

cut was to utilize old school cleansing methods to help my sprit feel

better. Speaking of which, I need to take a cleansing bath and go to

bed. I run the water as hot as I can stand it and pour sweet milk, honey,

and rose petals into the tub. This is one of my most favorite bath

prescriptions. Oshune's bath of attraction always makes me feel better.

I sink into the concoction and allow the ingredients to permeate

all of my senses. The plastic pillow squeezes a bit of air out as I rest my

head and relax into the steamy room.

*"You know you'll never be with that boy for long, or any other boy,*

*for that matter," Esmeralda says, interrupting my private moment.*

I cover my ears as if it'll stop her shrill voice from entering my

head. "Please God, not again."

*"You can pray out loud all you like, but it won't help a bit. It's part of*

*the Williams' Women's legacy. You can have a happy marriage, or a*

*happy priesthood, but you cannot have both."*

*"That's not always the case, Esmeralda."*

*"Are you sure about that, little Jayd? I haven't read the entire spirit book, but I know enough about your lineage to know that the only priestesses who ever had happy marriages at some point had to give up their crowns."*

She does have a point but I refuse to believe that it's an either/or situation. I can have both, can't I?

*"Perhaps they were just with the wrong people."* I think that if Mama would've married Dr. Whitmore she could've had the best of both worlds.

*"Perhaps the choice was never theirs to make, thus the curse of your legacy, child."*

*"We are not cursed!" I wish I knew how to shut this trick up. It's bad enough I had to give up precious wake hours to her when she was alive, but now that she's dead I have to give up good sleep, too. Will I ever catch a break?*

*"A break? Ha! Maybe you're not ready to be queen after all."*

Again, Esmeralda leaves my thoughts abruptly. She can laugh at my request all she wants to, but I know that there has to be a way to own my powers and chill, too.

Yesterday was the busiest Friday that we've had at Netta's in a long time. And with Mama and Netta barely speaking after their blow up, it's been unusually tense when Mama does decide to show up. I just want to get through the rest of this weekend without completely losing it. Hopefully Esmeralda will leave me be from now on. I have enough to think about without her random drop-ins disturbing my sanity.

*"What do you have going on this fine Saturday afternoon?"* my mom asks, invading my privacy. I'm having a hard enough time figuring out what to wear without her all up in my head.

*"I'm going to Natasia's wedding shower,"* I say, eyeing my skinny jeans, cream pumps and matching tank. All I need is my mom's short jean jacket, and this outfit should work.

*"Oh, that sounds like fun. Is a lesbian's wedding shower the same as a straight woman's or no?"* My mom can be so silly sometimes.

*"Mom, I don't know, but Natasia's still very much a woman. I'm sure they're very similar,"* I think back. I search through her barren closet

and there's no sign of the jacket.

"*Okay, if you say so. Take notes for my shower, Jayd. You've got to help your Aunt Vivica with ideas. I don't want it to be boring.*"

"*I'll see what I can do.*" I walk into the living room and hope it's inside of the smaller closet in there. "Mom, where's your jean jacket?" I ask, verbally. There are only boxes of old tax returns and other papers with no clothes in sight.

"*On my back. Why?*"

"*Why are all of your clothes disappearing? Now I have to change my outfit, again.*"

"*Girl, please. Do I have Macy's written on my closet doors? Besides, you need to get used to the fact that I won't be living there for too much longer, Jayd. What are you going to do when I move out for good?*"

"*I don't know.*" Between Mama's return to wifedom and my mom's impending wedding, I'm not sure where I fit into either of their lives.

"*Well, you'd better start thinking about it, and hard. You'll have to do all of your own shopping, and not in my closet. Have fun at the shower, and tell Nigel I said hey.*"

"*Will do.*"

I feel like I'm being forced into adulthood way too fast. I'd better get a move on if I don't want to miss the bus to Nigel's neck of the woods.

"Jayd, you made it," Natasia says. She and her fiancé are in matching white pants suits and they're both glowing. Good to see that someone's love life is blossoming. Maybe there's some hope for true, lasting love after all.

"Of course. I wouldn't miss this for the world." I hug Natasia and then pass the shower gift to her hostess.

"This is Blair, one of our Spelman sisters and also my Maid of Honor," Natasia says, introducing the plain looking yet immaculately dressed young woman. "And you remember, Regina, my fiancé."

"Welcome," Regina says, kissing me on the cheek. Her hair's shorter than it was the last time I saw her and she's still rocking it blonde. They're a stunning couple.

"Come on in. We're about to serve lunch outside." Blair ushers me toward the patio.

"Sounds like I came at just the right time." I walk across the crowded living room smiling and nodding to various strangers before stepping outside out onto the deck where I encounter several familiar faces.

"I'm sorry, Ms. Jackson. I am for real!" Chase says, mimicking

*Outkast.* I'm still a bit pissed at his reunion with Alia, but I can't be mad at my boy forever. It's not his fault he doesn't remember that what we had was so much better than what he and Alia have any day.

"What's up, y'all?" I ask, realizing that I missed the real party. Rah and Trish nod in response, both looking as faded as Chase sounds.

"Now it's an official party," Nigel says, wrapping his arms around my body as he steps behind me, reeking of herb. "Heard from your girl yet?"

"No, Nigel, and you know if I do I'll tell you." I'm so tired of him asking me about Mickey. I want to know where she and G took my goddaughter just as much as he does. Unfortunately, the official word on the street is that they disappeared.

Rah looks at me, doubtful. "You sure about that? The Jayd I used to know was very loyal to her people."

"Used to know?" I look from him to Trish and suck my teeth.

"I'm just saying, your hair isn't the only thing that's changed about you lately."

"Okay, you two," Chase says, waving hands like he's officiating a fight. "Back to your separate corners. It's a happy day."

Chase is right. If it weren't Natasia's day I'd check this fool right where he and his phony ass wifey sit.

85

"You sure can ruin a good high, Jayd. Damn." No this trick didn't fix her lips to speak to me sideways. Trish had better check herself before she gets punked in front of all these lovely people.

Before I can respond, Mr. Esop follows the caterers out of the kitchen door and directs the food placement. That's usually his wife's job, who's noticeably absent from the festivities.

"Nigel, where's your mom?" I ask, looking around the crowded yard for my former mentor.

"Locked in her room where she's been since Mickey disappeared," Nigel says. "You know she wasn't feeling a party today, especially not celebrating a marriage she's still denying's going to happen a few weeks from now."

"What's the date?" Trish asks, looking at Rah. She's unusually chatty today. What the hell? I like the silent Trish better.

"New Year's Day. They want to start off the year as wife and wife."

"That sounds like a good day to get married. What do you think, Rah?"

Why is Trish asking him about wedding dates? We're all under the legal age in California, no matter how desperate she is to legally lock his ass down.

"I like to be original," Rah grimaces. Is he seriously considering marrying her just to keep full custody of Rahima? He didn't mention that during his impromptu visit the other day.

"Why'd you cut your hair?" Trish asks. This is the most she's ever spoken to me in one sitting and I don't like it. She's getting to comfortable with my crew.

"It wasn't my choice."

Mr. Esop makes his way over to our table, all smiles. At least one of Natasia's parents is happy for her and Regina. "Please, eat," Mr. Esop says. The brown liquor he's sipping on has got his eyes almost as red as his son's. "We've got quite a spread."

"I can see that," I say, admiring the New Orleans themed menu. "Creole food. My favorite."

"Regina's, too," Natasia says, guiding her fiancé by the hand to our table. "Her people are originally from the Bayou."

"Really?" Chase asks. "I didn't know folks in New York came from down south."

"There aren't many but yes, there are a few of us speckled about. I hear you're also from there," Regina says to me. What else has Natasia told her fiancé about me? She doesn't know a lot of my secrets, but she knows enough.

"Actually my grandmother is. I'm Straight out of Compton."

"Just like Easy E." Chase is silly enough when he's sober. Once he's high, he's just a damned fool.

"Okay, enough talking. Time to get our eat on, my friends." Nigel stands and rubs his hands on his chiseled abs.

"Agreed. I'm going to wash my hands first." I stand and walk back into the house.

Of course both of the downstairs bathrooms are occupied. I head upstairs to use one of those. I'll also take the opportunity to check on Mrs. Esop while I'm up there. I wish that I could say that there are no hard feelings between us, but we're both too real for such pretenses. My time spent as her unwilling protégé wasn't all bad, but her intentions weren't always the best, and that shit got old fast.

On my way out of the bathroom Rah corners and then pulls me into the hallway. So much for checking on Mrs. Esop.

"So, those dreams that we shared meant nothing to you?" He's a little too close for my comfort.

"Seriously, Rah? You're the one planning the youngest wedding in Cali ever with Trish. Is she knocked up yet, or do you really believe that she's down for simply being a stepmother forever?"

Rah backs up. "What do you mean by that?"

"Don't play dumb, Rah. You don't wear it well."

"It's not like I just go around getting chicks pregnant, Jayd. If that were the case, you'd be carrying my baby right, or at least in our dreams."

"Thank God they're just dreams." They're very realistic, but I'm grateful they're not real. I don't think I could handle it if we ever made love in reality.

"Really, Jayd? Are you thankful about how things between us have worked out, or didn't work out?" Rah asks, resuming his original stance. I should've escaped when I had the chance. "From what I've seen, we could've been good together. But I didn't need a psychic vision to tell me that. I've always known that shit."

"And how does Trish feel about your feelings for me?"

"Shit, she knows it too. Anybody who's ever been in the same room with us can feel our vibe. It's too strong to deny."

"What are you two doing up here?" Mrs. Esop asks, shocking us both.

Rah backs up. "We're just talking, Mrs. E."

"He's talking. I needed to use the bathroom, and the two downstairs were occupied."

"Well, Jayd, just make yourself at home then, why don't you?" Damn. She's really not feeling me anymore. I hate that she's my enemy now, but she can't mess with Mama and expect to be cool with me.

"Rah, would you be a dear and tell my husband or my son to please bring me a plate. No one's even asked if I'd like to sample the food from my own caterer being served in my own home."

"You could come downstairs, Mrs. E," Rah offers. "It's a beautiful day, and I'm sure Natasia would love it if you'd join us."

"No thank you, dear. I can see the day perfectly fine from my private patio. And something to drink, too." Mrs. Esop returns to her room.

"Yes, Mrs. E."

"Thank you, dear. And Jayd, when your hoodrat friend contacts you, please send her my regards. I'm going to miss this little cat and mouse game when Mickey and her thug boyfriend are finally caught and thrown in jail like the criminals that they are. Enjoy the party."

Mrs. Esop closes the double doors to the master suite. I'm grateful for the intrusion, even if it was rude as hell.

"She's awfully chilly these days," I say as we head back downstairs.

"Yeah, like Alaska." Rah steps aside to let me go first. "I don't even think her husband can touch her she's so upset about everything."

"Poor Mr. Esop," I say, taking my time walking down the winding staircase. These pumps are not everyday wear for me. "She can't blame everyone for problems that are of her own making."

"This isn't on Mrs. Esop, Jayd. She didn't take the baby."

"The baby's not hers to take."

"Whatever, Jayd. You know Mickey's wrong for this shit, especially running away with G. Besides, she can't give Nickey the life she deserves, not with that nigga."

"It's not our call to make, Rah. Mickey's the mama. Even if she didn't make the best decision in this case, Nickey's still her daughter."

Rah looks at me, disappointed. "Now you see why I said you used to be down for your crew, no questions asked? Your loyalty's questionable, Jayd. What happened to you?"

"Where have you two been?" Trish asks from the bottom of the winding stairwell.

"Talking to Mrs. Esop." Rah reaches the bottom before me and kisses her forehead. "She wants a plate."

"And something to drink," I add, further enraging his wannabe baby-mama's already tense attitude. Whether he believes it or not, it's only a matter of time before she makes Rah a father of two or more.

"I'll get it for her," Trish says.

"I think she'd prefer it if Nigel or his dad got it, but thanks for offering." Rah looks at me, disappointed.

"Of course, babe. Anything for family, right?" Trish says.

"Precisely, baby."

Whatever. They walk off hand-in-hand and I follow, only because I want my plate. I hate simple bitches, especially thirsty ones. Trish is as thirsty as they come, but I have to admit, she always finds a way to get what she wants. In this case, she wants to wife Rah up, and I think she's working all of her magic to make that wish come true.

*"The same women who smile at you will also secretly plot your demise."*
*–Netta*
*Drama High, volume 17: Sweet Dreams*

## ~6~
## BB

After attending the shower yesterday and then working all morning today, I'm physically and emotionally wiped out. Fortunately, my mom had some sympathy on me and left her fiancé's car here for the night. It was more selfish in action, though, but I'll take what I can get. They went to Vegas for the night and didn't want to leave the car parked on the street at his apartment building. Unlike here, he doesn't have covered parking. It doesn't matter, really. Our car still gets broken into on a regular basis. At least there's no risk of parking tickets.

I should clean my hair tools scattered about everywhere, but I need a nap before I can move another muscle. My sleep has been jacked up lately, to say the least. Hopefully Esmeralda will take the day off and let me get in some good dreams of my own, without her—or Rah for that matter—intruding. Tonight I'll catch up on The Daily Show. Noah Trevor always helps me sleep better.

*"You are definitely your grandmother's child," the crippled, old man says. I can't see his face, but his voice is shaky, his back's bent in a permanent curve, and the skin on his hands is wrinkled.*

*"Yes, I am."*

*"Then why don't you act like it? Here, I'll show you how."*

*He covers my hand with his own and forces me to look into his victim's eyes: It's Esmeralda. She's in a trance-like state, and sits upright in a large wooden chair. Her blue eyes are glossed over and she seems to be paralyzed.*

*"What are you doing to her?" I ask, my voice frantic with fear.*

*"Preparing her for you, of course, my queen."*

*"But I don't want her. And I didn't ask you to do any of this."*

*"No, you didn't. But it's my job to open one door and close another, whether or not you ask me to. I perform the will of God. That's beyond your scope of expertise, no matter how powerful your crown may be. Your job is to take care of business."*

*"What am I supposed to do with her?"*

*"Borrow her sight, just like Queen Jayd would do."*

*I follow the old man's advice and snatch the vision right out of her eyes. I actually feel normal for first time in a very long time, until I realize that I'm in full possession of Esmeralda's site, which is painfully cold. Oh hell no. I can't take the pain.*

My cell rings with a call from an unknown caller pulling me out of the disturbing dream. Those calls usually go unanswered, but something's telling me to pick this one up.

"Hello?"

"Jayd, it's me." It's the call we've all been waiting for.

"Mickey?" I whisper, sitting up straight. "Are you and the baby okay? Where are you?"

"Open the door and find out."

I can hear footsteps quickly walking up the stairs. I kick of my blankets, jump off of the couch, and undo the multiple locks on my mom's front door.

"Mickey, where have you been?

"Jayd, look. I don't have time to explain. Just take the baby, please." She hands me a sleeping Nickey securely tucked into her car seat. "And tell Nigel and his bitch of a mama to back the hell off."

"Mickey, you've got to be joking. I'm not taking Nickey anywhere. She's your responsibility," I say, attempting to pass the baby back to her. "You need to come clean with Nigel and everyone else before you're in over your head."

"I can't do that, Jayd. Not after what happened at Esmeralda's," she says, rejecting the pass. "We're already in too deep."

"Mickey, what are you talking about?"

I can tell from the cracks in her voice that she's really scared, but it's not the law that's got her shook. "Rousseau scares the shit out of me, Jayd! I don't know who or what he is, but I'm more afraid of him than I am of G, and G scares the shit out of me most of the time."

"Mickey, don't worry about Rousseau. He can't hurt you anymore."

"That's a bunch of crap, Jayd and you know it." Mickey glances over her shoulder and down the stairs like Rousseau can hear her in Compton from Inglewood. "Even them fools from Sin Piedad broke out after he came outside and confronted us. He ain't right, Jayd. I'm telling you. There's something wrong with that dude."

"Agreed, but he's not your biggest problem at the moment, Mickey." I hand Mickey her daughter who begins to squirm in her sleep.

Mickey takes the handle of the seat and stares at her baby. Tears well up in her eyes. "I know he's not. Nigel and his mama are. If they can find me that means that dude will find me, and I can't let that happen. Here," Mickey says, handing Nickey off to me once more. "I'll be back for her. In the meantime, do what you have to do to keep her safe, please."

"Mickey, no. Don't do this!" I yell after her but it's no use. I can't run down the stairs with Nickey in tow as quickly as she can.

"I can't," Mickey says without looking back. "I don't have a choice. Please keep her safe, Jayd. As her godmother it's your job, right?"

Before I can answer Mickey disappears down the driveway. Damn it. With Nickey still asleep, I carry her inside and lock the door behind us. My first call is to her daddy.

"What up, girl?" Nigel answers, sounding half asleep. It's not that late, but late enough for most of my folks to be in chill mode, like I was before my surprise guest appeared.

"Can you come over to my mom's apartment, please?"

"Did you hear from Mickey?" Suddenly he sounds wide-awake. "Do you know where she is with my baby girl?"

"I don't know where Mickey is, but Nickey's here with me sleeping in her car seat."

"I'm on my way."

"We'll be here."

"Oh, and Jayd. Thank you."

"Of course, Nigel. No matter what Rah said yesterday, you know I'll always have your back, and my goddaughter's best interest at heart."

"I know that," Nigel says. I can hear him moving around in the background. "Rah's just scared of losing Rahima to Sandy. After going through this bull with my baby-mama I feel him. Trust me, Jayd. At the end of the day, Rah knows who you are and how much you mean to both of us."

"If you say so." Rah was dead serious about me changing from his neighborhood homegirl to some chick he doesn't know or trust anymore.

"I do. See you in a min."

"Ok."

"On second thought, Jayd. Do you mind meeting me at Simply Wholesome in thirty minutes? This whole thing sounds suspiciously easy to me, don't you think?"

"You're being paranoid but I can't blame you. I wouldn't put anything pass G." Nigel's lucky I happen to have access to a car tonight. Otherwise he'd be trekking from Lafayette Square to Larch Street.

"You got a ride?"

"Yeah. I'll get her there safely."

"Thank you." Nigel ends the call.

"Guess it's just me and you for a little while, baby girl."

Mama used to say that there's nothing more precious than a sleeping baby. I agree. I carefully set the car seat down next to the couch. Half of me wants to step out in the yoga pants, t-shirt and house slippers I'm wearing and just throw on a coat, but the Oshune in me won't let that happen.

"I'll be right back. Hope you're having sweet dreams."

As soon as I let go of the handle Nickey begins to stir. Seems like she's become accustomed to being rocked to sleep. I'm sure Mrs. Esop will be happy to further indulge that sleep association.

Nickey wakes up and locks onto my sight. She's getting real good at using her powers on me.

*"Thank Goddess you found me! It's about time, Godmama Jayd. You can be real slow when you want to be, huh?"*

*"It's nice to see you too, Nickey,"* I think back. This little psychic queen has the sass of someone fifty years her elder. *"And I didn't find you. Your mother brought you to me, little Miss."* I unstrap her and hug her firmly. I don't think I could've missed her more if she were my own baby.

*"Well, it's about time that she did something right. You don't want to know what I've been through these past few days. Her and that dude are cray-cray, for real!"*

"Don't talk about your mother that way," I say, returning her to the secure seat.

*"Hey, truth is truth. The two of them together is more than a notion. They set each other off like a lighter to a firecracker. My mom's tripping if*

*she thinks that he's going to help us at all. All G wants is to control her, and*

*I've had enough."*

"What do you mean you had enough?" I ask out loud while

changing clothes in my mom's room. I take a quick glance in the

bathroom mirror and smooth my short ponytail back. Anyone who looks

at me can tell that I was knocked out ten minutes ago even it is only

eight o'clock.

*"It's like I said, they were tripping and needed some reasoning. So,*

*while my mama was sleeping I snuck into her head and gave her one hell*

*of a nightmare."*

*"Nickey, no."* Although I'm ticked at her for using her untamed

powers on her mother, I can't help but be a little proud. She's getting

pretty good with her sight.

*"Nickey, yes! I had to get out of there, Godmama Jayd. You just don't*

*know. The things I've witnessed, no child should ever see!"*

*"Okay, Nickey. I don't need details. We've got to get out of here.*

*Your daddy should be at Simply Wholesome soon."*

*"Sounds good. I could use some lentil soup and a chicken patty. A*

*sistah's hungry, and all they fed me was that stupid bottle."*

*"You are a baby, Nickey."* I lock the closed door behind us, and

head downstairs. Lugging around a baby in this contraption is good

birth control.

*"Hey, I can eat soup. These gums work well on soft things. There are*

*lots of babies who eat real food, not that cloudy formula they shake up for*

*me. Yuck!"*

*"Okay, okay. Soup it is."* I open the back passenger side door and

lock her in. We could both use a snack.


Why did Nigel choose here of all places to meet on a Sunday

night? It's packed with all of the usual suspects. Anywhere else

would've been better, but I feel him about feeling like a set-up courtesy

of G. In his mind, it was too easy. And my mom's hood isn't the hottest

place in Inglewood or South Central, but it's hot enough. Last summer I

saw a dude get shot by rival gang members after I walked to the liquor

store, so I can't be mad. Enough people know Nigel to both have his

back, and be a potential enemy.

By the time I find my way inside it's too late to turn around. I spot

Nellie standing in line while her man, David, and my estranged friend,

Keenan are talking on the outside patio. Shit. The last thing that I need is another confrontation with Keenan over David's trifling, hypocritical ass. At least Summer's not here. She takes Sundays off to attend Agape, her church of choice.

"OMG. Is that Nickey?" Nellie asks, bending down to greet the smiling baby. "Look how much she's grown."

"Yeah, babies tend to do that." I set the seat down and take a menu from the counter. "How have you been?" I ask, trying to remain civil with her sometimey self.

I never know when this chick is going to flip on me, but she usually behaves herself when she's one-on-one. It's her rich, white girl clique that tends to bring out the worst in her.

"Okay." Nellie's unusually covered up on a nice night. Thanks to global warming it's a humid evening, and she's wearing a turtleneck, leggings, and boots. What the hell?

"Nellie, I can't help you if you don't want it."

"It's not always bad, Jayd." Nellie looks back outside at David chat it up with Keenan.

"It never is with a crazy person," I snap back. Nellie sounds too much like every delusional woman defending her abuser in the name of love.

"David's not crazy, Jayd," Nellie says. "He's been diagnosed with bipolar disorder. It's a real illness."

"Is he being treated for it?" I ask, already knowing the answer. Nellie's silence confirms it. "Until David gets help, he might as well just be any other crazy jerk running around beating on his girlfriend. I never thought you'd be one of those chicks, Nellie."

"That's very sensitive, Jayd," Nellie says, flipping her fresh weave over her right shoulder. "Real classy."

"I do have sympathy, Nellie. For you, not David. He's not trying to help himself at all and you know it. Until then, he's a dangerous bully, and you're enabling his behavior."

Unbeknownst to Nellie, Nickey nods her head in agreement. At least she's feeling me.

"Look, Iyanla. I don't need another one of your lectures. We're working it out, between us," she says, pointing at David and then back to herself. "Get your own man, and then you can tell other people what to do in their relationships."

Well, damn. I guess this basic bitch just told me.

"Ready?" David says, claiming their order. With his free hand he puts his index finger in the middle of her back and pushes her toward the exit.

"Very." Nellie looks down at Nickey one last time and then up at me without saying another word.

"Bye, Nellie," I say, after them. "And David, I'll tell Nigel you send your regards."

He turns around and shoots me a look that causes the hairs on my arms to stand. Good. He should feel like the cowardly jerk that he is. I hope Nellie comes to her senses and soon. Love shouldn't require dealing with someone's rage, not at the expense of her own safety.

"I'm still waiting for an apology, you know," Keenan says, sneaking up behind me. "Not that it really hurt, but that slap was completely uncalled for."

"Was it really, Keenan?"

"Violence is never the answer, Jayd."

"Tell that to your boy, David."

"Don't you mean your boy, Nigel?" Keenan says, referring to the ass whooping David received after hitting Nellie.

"He was defending our friend."

"That's not what Nellie and David said."

"The truth always comes to the surface, Keenan."

"Yes, I suppose it does," he says, looking down at Nickey who rolls her eyes at him. I love my spunky godbaby. "Whatever the case, I hope this goes away quietly for Nigel's sake. UCLA's not going to touch him with an assault charge on his record. Anyhow, I'm late for work." Keenan claims his to-go order and leaves a tip in the jar. "Drop by the coffee house when you get a min. Nice haircut, by the way. Later."

"Enjoy," I say. I eye the menu again and decide on our food. I'm getting hungry and by the look on Nickey's face, I can tell she's ready to eat, too.

Nigel should've been here by now. He's not answering my texts or calls. It's been twenty minutes since I arrived and I'm starting to worry. Nickey happily ate her soup, and I even gave her a few nibbles from my patty. The girl can eat. Her mother didn't even leave a diaper

106

bag. Just one diaper, a bottle and a few wipes in the seat with her. I already changed her diaper once. If her daddy doesn't get here soon I'm going to have to walk across the street to *CVS* for some supplies.

"Nickey," Nigel says, jogging from the front door to our table in the first row. I wanted her to be the first thing he saw when he got here and it worked.

I can see his dad's Benz parked out front with both of his parents waiting.

"Sorry we're so late. My mom insisted on getting her a new car seat and other supplies for the ride home."

"That's okay. Ten more minutes and we would've been stuck with the clean up crew." The Sunday staff has been prepping for closing, which is at nine on Sundays. "She does need some basics, though. What she has on her is what she came with."

"You know we've got that covered. Thank you, Jayd. Really. You don't know how much this means to me. I promised her I'd take care of her for her daddy, Tre, saving my life and I meant that. His baby is my baby. And we're going home to stay this time."

"I'm just happy that she's back safe and sound."

Mrs. Esop reaches across the steering wheel where her husband sits in the driver's seat and presses on the horn.

"You know my mom can't wait to see the baby. Bye, Jayd. See you at school in the morning." He kisses my cheek, picks up a contented Nickey, and heads out.

"Tell your parents I said goodnight, Nigel."

I know Nickey will be spoiled and loved. I'm almost jealous of the little princess. Her life is about to change for the better, and I'm glad I could help a little bit with that. Now if I could just help myself out that would be fantastic.

*"If I never challenge myself -even when it's not necessarily my thing- I'll
never grow, and that's what I'm here for."*
*- Jayd*
*Drama High, volume 12: Pushin'*

~ 7 ~
# SPLIT PERSONALITY

After school yesterday I came straight home and worked all night

filling client's orders. Mama's the epitome of not giving a care about

anything or anyone else but her and her man at the moment. This is so

backwards and I can't explain it. However, her clients seem pleased

with my work, so I'm going to keep it moving and stop worrying about

what others do as much as possible. And, with Nickey safely at Nigel's,

at least that's another worry off my mind.

Once I was done with Mama's clients, I started doing some

research on how to help my own out, including Jeremy. His issue is a bit

more complicated because this is the second time I've appealed to the

Orisha and ancestors on his behalf, and they don't really like it when

petitioners don't listen the first time around. In order to work on

Jeremy's new case I have to be creative in my approach.

The main thing is to free him from his fake wifey's clutches, and

that means doing work on her, too. There was one passage in the spirit

book about effectively killing off jealous broads that seemed really

effective. Since it's safe to say that this is how her hold over him started,

I thought I'd start there first and rid him of her and Esmeralda's wickedness before moving on to his legal troubles. Maybe the ancestors will have sympathy on him if we work on it from a position of love gone wrong first, and then appeal to the Orisha to move the direction of his legal case in his favor. There's always so much work to do. Jeremy had better be prepared to pay me generously for this because I'm done working for free.

When Lexi and I make it to the spirit room we realize that someone's beat us to the punch this morning.

"Mama, what are you doing back here so early?" I ask as I make my way across the intimate kitchen and into the main room where the shrines are housed. I had to leave the gris-gris for Jeremy on them overnight before finishing it. I'll take care of the last step on the way to school.

"Morning, baby," Mama says, barely looking up from the spirit book.

"What are you working on? I thought I finished all of the clients' orders last night."

"You did, baby. And thank you for that. But this is personal work."

"Is it anything that I can help you with?" I check the opened mojo bag with Jeremy's name written on the outside and sprinkle some altar water on it before wrapping it up and safely tucking it inside of my bra. I have to get some of my own ashe on it if I want it to work right.

"No, Jayd, but thank you for the offer. After years of working on other folks' problems, I've decided to focus on myself and my relationship."

By the ingredients spread out on the tall kitchen table, I can tell that Mama's fixing all kinds of mojo bags and potions to keep daddy faithful. Oh shit, what happened already. One minute they're in marital bliss, and the next Mama's working before sunrise to help Daddy keep all eyes on her.

"Mama, you've always told me that the best way to help myself is by helping those I love. Let me help you. Can some of this wait until I get back from school?"

"I told you, I got this," Mama snaps back. "You're a seventeen-year old girl who knows nothing about love or the real world. How can you possibly think that you could help me, a grown-ass married woman who's had more lifetimes than you could ever imagine?"

*"Well, that was uncalled for,"* my mom says, taking the thought right out of my mind. *"I've never seen her this nervous about Daddy before.*

*"I know, right? She's straight tripping this morning."*

"Why are you just standing there?" Mama says, passing me by to place a few of her objects on the shrine. Guess I'm not the only one appealing to our ancestors for help. "Don't you have school to get to?"

"Mama, did something happen?" I ask, thoroughly concerned about her mental state. She seems on edge and upset.

"Jayd, I already told you. This is grown woman's business. You're far from being able to assist in matters of the heart, baby."

"I'm not a baby, Mama. In case you forgot, you've entrusted me with your personal clients, and they are all well grown with problems of their own. Furthermore, I haven't heard one complaint yet. Have you?"

*"Oh hell, Jayd,"* my mom says. *"You're about to get it now. I can't listen to my baby get cussed out by my mother. Be strong, little girl. I'll check in with you later."*

So much for my mom having my back, spiritually or otherwise. She's right: I am out of line, but so is my grandmother. And personally,

I've had enough of her blind selfishness. She and Netta are still not on good terms, and now she's trying to make me out to be some sort of incompetent toddler. I'm not having it, not after all of the slack I've picked up on her behalf.

Mama turns away from the shrines and steps up to me, standing a few inches above my five-foot frame, but I'm not afraid. "What did you just say to me, little girl?" Mama's emerald eyes shimmer in anger.

"I said that I'm not a baby. If I'm grown enough to do your work for you, then I'm grown enough to be shown some respect and not dismissed when you're in a bad mood."

Out of nowhere, Mama slaps me across the face. The force of her hit is so powerful that it knocks me into the shrine. All of the accouterments crash to the carpet along with my body. I don't remember the last time Mama hit me, but it wasn't nearly as hard as she just did.

"Don't bite the hand that feeds you, Jayd," Mama says, unapologetically. "Never forget your place with me, is that understood? I told you a long time ago that you have too much of your mother's spirit in you. It's not going to serve you well, especially not when dealing with me. I'd advise you to check yourself here and now, little girl, before you end up like her: powerless."

Mama storms out of the spirit room with Lexi hot on her trail. She leaves me behind to clean up the mess, and myself, from the floor.

*"That's the Mama I know and fear,"* my mom says, compassionately. *"I'm sorry you had to see that side of her. I thought the Erzulie Freda side of Oshune was buried long ago, but ever since Esmeralda died there's an imbalance in Mama's world, whether she wants to admit it or not."*

*"Well, I for one wish she'd find a way to balance it all, and not with Daddy's assistance because he's bound to disappoint her again."* I pick myself up off of the rug and look at the mess we created.

*"You're right about that, which means you're wise beyond your years, Jayd. Mama knows the truth, even if she's in denial. I love you, honey. You better get going before you're late for school. The mess can wait til later."*

*"Bye, mom. Have a good day."*

*"You too, baby."*

While retrieving some of the fallen sacred items that can't wait until later, I notice the inside of one of the mojos that I never thought to utilize in my own work has St. John the Conqueror's root in it. I remember the old witchdoctor that Mama occasionally works with in Long Beach uses it regularly, but Mama not as much.

"Maybe this is the trick to put my work into high gear," I say to our shrines.

If Mama's going to act like a spoiled brat in love, I have to completely take matters into my own hands, without my grandmother's approval or help. When I get back from working at Netta's this afternoon I'll get right on it. At this moment, my stomach's growling and I need to get a move on if I don't want to miss my bus.

I'm so done helping Mama clean up her slack. She can have it. If her business goes to hell with gasoline drawers on, then so be it. I'm tired of trying to help those who refuse to earnestly help themselves, my grandmother included. What am I, her lackey? Oh, hell no. I refuse. I'm no one's helpless second. I have my own business to take care of, clients included, and I intend to let Jeremy know that this time my services will cost more than a kiss. Affairs of the heart don't pay the bills, and his tab has officially run out.

When I step outside, Lexi's dutifully manning the door, as always. At least someone's loyal to me. I know she's tripping because of her owner's unpredictability, but she's not going anywhere, and I can respect that.

We head to the main house and through the back door. Lexi lazily takes her customary spot under the kitchen table. She looks like I feel: deserted by her best friend. Luckily there's a box of Cornflakes on top of the refrigerator. That will have to work for breakfast. I won't even waste anymore time looking for milk.

"Hey, niecey. What's good with you?" Bryan says, walking into the kitchen from his night job. He looks as tired as I feel, minus the sore face.

"Same bull, different morning." I grab a piece of bread from the opened bag on the table and a banana to accompany my dry cereal.

"Breakfast of champions, I see," he says, making light of my situation. I'm too hungry to be picky. Last night's dinner was noodles and broccoli, so this is right in alignment with my standards. I miss waking up at Chase's house, for more reasons than one.

"You could always bring your favorite niece breakfast when you come in early, since you care so much."

"I could, or you could wake up and make sure that you get a good meal first thing in the morning," he says, sounding like his big sister. My mom's impending nuptials are already forcing changes on me that I'm not ready to deal with. "I'm telling you, when you get my age you'll wish you took better care of yourself early on."

"Bryan, please. You're not that much older than me."

"Whatever, chica. I'm still an old man."

"Since when are your mid-twenties old?"

"Since I became lactose intolerant." He retrieves his almond milk from the refrigerator. No one ever touches his food.

"Okay, way too much information," I say, stuffing the piece of bread into my mouth while tying my shoes. "What are you doing here anyway? I thought you and the girlfriend were shacking up permanently."

"Not yet, little girl. And stay out of grown folks' business," he says, yanking my hair. "What happened to your ponytail?"

"Misty."

My uncle nods in affirmation, remembering the epic battle. "It suits you. Short, sassy, and sweet." Bryan takes his bag of granola from the cabinet next to the stove and pours some into a bowl on the counter.

Maybe I should eat more like him, if for no other reason than his food's always in stock around here.

"I love you, too."

"Whatever, girl. Eat something when you get to school. I'll holla," Bryan says, heading into the living room with his breakfast.

I better hurry if I don't want to miss my first bus. My backpack's by the front door and so is my jacket. It still feels weird stepping onto the front porch and not encountering Esmeralda's cold, blue stare. Not that I miss her physical presence, but her absence will take some getting used to. I zip up my *North Face* Parka, an old gift from Jeremy, and sling my bag over my shoulder.

"Jayd, baby, just a minute," Mama says, creeping out of her room wearing a silk robe that I've never seen before. It's a far departure from the usual housedresses that she wears. I guess a new attitude comes with a new wardrobe, too.

Maybe she wants to apologize for the pimp slap she just laid on me.

"Listen, I need you to take care of this for me," she says, handing me a packet of herbs and a written request. "Mrs. Washington has been waiting for this for over a week, and I just don't have the time to deal with her manic behavior. Have a good day at school."

"Mama, are you serious?" I say, handing the ingredients back to her.

"Jayd, it's easy. Just follow the instructions on the other side of the request to the letter and you'll be fine. Then, call her and let her know when she can pick it up. It won't take you but an hour or two. Consider it part of your spirit lessons. Besides, after the way you just showed your ass, you owe me." Mama turns around and walks back toward her room, where I'm sure Daddy's waiting. Something inside of me refuses to let this go, even at the risk of getting hit again.

"No."

Mama tilts her neck to the right side in disbelief, and I can't blame her. I've never said no to my grandmother before, but this is an unreasonable request. Besides, I'm already picking up her slack at the shop. Why should I have to start taking on her private clients at home, too?

"What did you just say to me, little girl?" Mama puts both hands on her hips and again steps up to my face so close that I can smell the wine on her breath from last night.

"I said no, Mama. I have enough work to do, which already includes some of your work. I don't have time."

"Well then make time, young lady. You don't have a choice."

Why is she forcing my hand on this? I don't want to outright defy my grandmother but unfortunately she's leaving me little choice.

"Mama, what are you doing today?"

"Why?"

"Because I doubt you'll be at the beauty shop helping Netta, your business partner and best friend, remember her?"

"Netta can handle herself. Besides, the last time I was there I filled enough orders to last a couple of weeks for several of our most difficult clients."

"That's not the point, Mama, and you know it. You should be there. Actually, you should be here in your hustle state of mind, but instead you're running around after Daddy like a teenager, who, by the way still finds time to get his work done. I have to go."

Bryan looks on in silence. I'm sure the scene is familiar to him, and he choses to stay out of it.

"As usual, you're talking about shit that you know nothing about. My relationship with my husband has to take precedence over everything else, including my work."

"When it's good, right?" I say, reminding Mama of the reality of the situation. "I'm tired of your relationship drama. Whenever you and

Daddy decide to be happy, every one else is expected to fall into order. I'm sorry, Mama. This time, you're on your own."

"Jayd, you don't have a choice but to do as I say." Mama's eyes begin to glow as she locks onto my sight.

"Yes, I do. We've got serious business to handle, in both worlds. And neither are your priorities right now. Since when do you care what Daddy thinks about what we do?" I don't have time to play games, pimp slap be damned. I stare back at her with equal intensity, and to my surprise, she backs off. What the hell just happened?

"I've always cared. You'll understand once you have children, become a wife. If it's true love, you can't help but care."

"Love has nothing to do with us handling our business."

"Oh yes it does, little girl. When you love hard you will get hurt. Yet and still there's a lesson in the heartbreak every time." Mama walks outside toward the backhouse. I follow and head toward the back gate. What a morning.

*"Once you're in love you never really stop loving that person...It's just relationship shit, Jayd. That's all I can say about that."*
*–Netta,*
*Drama High, volume 17: Sweet Dreams*

~8~
# WHAT'S LOVE GOT TO DO WITH IT?

This weather's been so unpredictable lately. It's a brisk morning, but Mama's got my blood boiling. With my hoodie on, I begin my trek up the block. By the time I make it to Alondra Boulevard I notice a black Monte Carlo driving slowly behind me. I can turn and run if I feel danger, but for some reason I'm not threatened by the mysterious presence.

The car stops up ahead before I make it to my first bus stop a few feet away. The dark, tinted windows on the driver's side roll down and I see two familiar faces.

"Buenos dias, mami. Como estas?"

"Good morning to you, too, Javier. Good to see you, Mauricio," I say to both of Maggie's cousins. "Where have y'all been hiding?"

"In our ile, where you should have been too, mija."

I hear that. Nothing like one's spiritual house to protect you.

"You act like you didn't just commit the biggest crime of your life, little queen," Mauricio says. "Tell me, are you used to getting away with murder?"

It's nice not to have to hide myself from them. It also feels good being properly recognized for my spiritual accomplishments.

"No, not at all, actually. I really didn't kill her. It was my great-grandmother, to be honest. I was just her vessel."

"Yeah, okay. I get it. You're being all modest and shit. I can dig it," Javier says, looking me up and down. He's so sexy. Too bad he's too old for me, and a family man. "We're having a little get together this weekend. Abuela's cooking up a feast in celebration of our recent victory."

"We would be honored if you'd come, la reina." Who is Mauricio talking to?

"I'm no one's queen," I say, checking over my shoulder.

I know Mama's probably still in the house with Daddy, but I still fear her overhearing our conversation. I glance at my jade bracelets and consider removing them again. Even if I'm well out of earshot, Mama can still hear my thoughts when she wants to as long as I'm wearing these. I don't want her to think that I'm intentionally trying to usurp her power or position. If she'd get back on her game, we could all chill the hell out.

"Jayd, that's not true. Not at all," Javier says, seriously. "You're our queen, mami. We're here to serve and protect whenever you need it."

"Si. Consider us your royal knights in a shiny Monte Carlo," Mauricio says, forcing me to smile.

I blush at the compliment. "That's really sweet, you guys. But I'm good just being me—no knights needed." I check my phone for the time. The bus should be at the stop up ahead in two minutes. I'd better start walking if I don't want it to pass me by.

"Everybody needs protection, Jayd, even the toughest of queens."

"I keep telling you, I'm not the queen. That's my grandmother's title, not mine."

"That's not what I've been hearing around the block," Javier says. "Rumor has it that you're making quite a name for yourself. Again, we'd love to see you at the celebration. Let us you know if you need anything, anytime."

They pull off and I hot tail it up the block. It's interesting to think that I'm not the only one who knows that Mama's not the one doing all of the work around here. Maybe I should take her up on doing more work for her private clients since she's not taking the time to teach me anymore. I guess the only way that I'm going to master this shit is to take the initiative. In the meantime, let me catch this bus and get on with my school day. I'm sure that Netta will help me figure out the rest later.

The moment I stepped onto campus Jeremy questioned me about my work on his court case. Without disclosing all of the details, I had to let him know that I've got other priorities. He didn't need to know that I have a special gris-gris for him that I didn't get to finish making this morning due to the volatile fight with my grandmother. That's none of his business.

For some reason Jeremy's really starting to rub me the wrong way, and so is Alia. Cameron can have him, but Alia and Chase are working my nerves. She wasn't in class today and I'm grateful for it. I don't think I can take seeing her face. It just reminds me of what I could've had with Chase, and Jeremy's a constant reminder of what I had to sacrifice because of him. I've been hiding out for the entire lunch period, mostly because I have no one to hang with. Marcia's absent, and I assume that Alia and Chase are somewhere making out.

"Why so glum, chum?" Chase says, handing me a bottle of water.

My secret spot behind the drama room isn't so secret after all. He's always so thoughtful. I guess I assumed wrong about him and Alia.

"No reason. Well, nothing more than the usual." I gladly accept the cold drink and snack he offers me. "How's your day going?"

"It's going," Chase says, sitting down on the grass next to me. "Alia's under the weather so I'm going to take her some soup and OJ after school. Want to come?"

Hell no I don't want to accompany him to take care of a chick he wouldn't be with if he'd knew what we had going on.

"I think I'm good, but thanks anyway," I say, a bit saltier than I intend to be. I stand up to walk away before the bell for fifth period rings, and Chase follows.

"Jayd, what's up with you lately?" Chase steps in front of me and stops me from entering the classroom. "I feel like you're mad at me and I don't know what I did to piss you off."

His eyes are so sweet and honest. I hate lying to one of my best friends, but it's for his own good.

"It's nothing, Chase. I've got a lot going on. Don't worry about it."

"Of course I'm going to worry about it. You're my girl."

I wish that were true.

"Alia's your girl again, apparently. And I'm not your wingman. That's what Jeremy and Nigel are for." I step around him and enter the empty room.

Today we get to choose our final play for the semester. I've been out of it lately and my acting game has suffered because of it. I need to get back on track because I'm doing a horrible job pretending at the moment. Chase can see right through my tough girl act.

"Wait a minute. I only invited you because I know you two are friends, not because I needed a wingman. I'd never use you like that."

Chase doesn't deserve the shade I'm throwing at him. At the same time, in all honesty, I'm not sure that I can control it and keep from telling him the truth. It's one or the other, and as long as Esmeralda and Rousseau are still threats to us all I can't let that happen.

"Chase, just forget that I said anything. It's not you, okay? There's just so much going on in my life that it's really got me stressed out."

"Tell me about it," he says, removing his baseball cap and rubbing his close-cut shave. "I'm so stressed I don't even remember Mickey and her ex-dude running off with the baby."

Damn, Netta went hard on checking his memory from the night that Esmeralda almost made him one of her loyal servants—maybe too hard.

"It happens." More students file into the room. Usually I'm not happy to see most of my classmates but today is an exception. This conversation is becoming very uncomfortable.

"Am I missing something?" Chase asks, confused. "I feel like I have amnesia, or at the very least that I've been roofied. I can't remember much after that night at the beach."

He can't remember everything that happened that night, either. I made sure of that.

"I mean, I don't think I've lost time or anything," Chase continues, lowering his voice. "I can't explain it, really. It feels like I'm dreaming or something."

"It'll pass, Chase. Sometimes I get the same feeling, especially when I haven't slept well."

"I bet you do. By the way, my mom wants you to check in with her sooner than later, you feel me?"

"Yeah, I feel you." And I always will.

Mrs. Carmichael probably wants to talk to me about the fact that I abruptly moved out of her home, and about her son's selective amnesia. I can't take any more interrogations, especially when I'm wearing my heart on my sleeve. Our chat will have to wait until I get my game face back on, or at the very least until I can pretend to be okay with all of my recent sacrifices for the good of my friends and family. Until then I will have to keep faking it until I make it.

~ 9 ~
# DOLLED UP

The school day didn't improve much. The class voted to do *Alice in Wonderland* for the end of the year play. Without hesitation, I already know the main reason is because Alice is a little white girl. I'm still going to audition, of course. But if history is an accurate predictor, I already know what the outcome will be.

Chase was on his cell texting Alia all period long. I hate that they're back together, and the worst part is, he has no idea what I'm going through. I can't share it with anyone. It feels like I'm breaking up with myself, by myself. The only person that I can talk to about it is Netta. Mama doesn't remember what happened to Chase and isn't in the frame of mind to think about anyone else's love life but her own.

Mama and I didn't speak two words to each other at work, but neither did she and Netta for that matter. I started to tell Netta about me and Mama's fallout this morning, but decided against it. She's already upset with her best friend. The last thing I want to do is add fuel to that fire. I'm sure that she could tell the energy between me and my grandmother was thick. However, it's been that way since Mama started tripping, so nothing's too out of the ordinary where she's concerned. Besides, Netta's the only person I can talk about Chase with. I'd much rather spend my time talking about him than my family drama.

"Oh, Jayd. I feel your pain, girl. Chase was a sweet one, wasn't he?" Netta says, wiping down the hot combs. She barely got a break today. Mama left early to go grocery shopping with Daddy, and Netta didn't try to stop her. I think she's done arguing with her best friend.

"Yes, he was." I rinse the last few rollers in the sink and begin to replace them individually in the steamer slots. "How come I can't keep the good ones?" I refuse to believe Esmeralda's warning about the William's women curse.

"That's not the case, sweetie. You have to be patient. The right one will come along at the right time, and you'll never have to let him go."

"I don't know about that, Netta. There are plenty of single women out there who repeat that same mantra daily."

Nellie used to be into those books with rules about dating and shit like that. Yes, she did get a man finally, but I don't envy the one she got.

"Don't think like that, Jayd, or you most certainly will not attract your right man."

"As if there is a right man." I move on to the laundry and take it out to the back porch to wash. There's always more than enough work to do around here, but now that Mama's slacking, there's even more than usual. I feel like Cinderella around here more often than not. "The only ones I seem to attract come with a whole lot of drama."

"I know it seems like that right now, Jayd. Believe me when I say that it will get better. You'll see." Netta sounds more optimistic than usual.

"I think I'm good for the time being, Netta. Dudes have been nothing but a distraction so far."

"That's the smartest thing I think you've said all evening," Netta says, looking my way. "Until you're ready, I think that's the wisest course of action. Leave these young men alone in the meantime and in between time. You've got enough on your plate as it is."

Should I tell her about Esmeralda's presence in my dreams or just leave that to myself? I need some sort of reference but I think she'd go ballistic if she knew about my private counselor. I'm not anti-everything that my ancestor is saying, but I also know that Esmeralda never does anything purely out of the goodness of her heart, even if she doesn't currently possess one.

"What are you over there thinking about, young queen?"

"Nothing much," I lie. "I need to start planning my mom's bridal shower. I haven't had time to do it yet. I went to Natasia's last weekend and got some good ideas, though."

"Nigel's mama must be having the conniption fit of her life right about now."

"Not really." I take the clean clothes out of the drier and replace them with wet ones, ready for yet another load.

"When's the last time you did a head cleansing or took a spiritual bath, chile?"

"I've been taking my baths, but it seems like forever since I had a rogacion de cabeza." No wonder my head's been so hot lately.

"Lynn Mae is really on one, isn't she?" Netta hisses under her breath. "Here, baby. Let's cool that head off right now. It'll help with everything you're going through."

"Yes. Let's."

"Here, Jayd. Grab three towels from the cabinet and have a seat in the first wash chair. I'll prepare the rogacion while you say your prayers. Meditate on being cool."

There are plenty of clean, white towels to help with the traditional ceremony. Luckily we're done with our clients for the day. I miss Mama being here during our quiet time at the shop. We used to do these types of ceremonies almost daily when I first became an iyawo. Like Netta

133

said, Mama's been on one, and my year of being a new priestess will be up before we know it.

"Here, baby. Lean back and let's wash that pretty little head of yours." Netta pours the concoction over my head and into the sink.

Initially the cool, fragrant water shocks my system. After a few moments, the cold feels good and calms my spirit. Thank God for my godmother. Without Netta I don't know what I'd do.

*"You'd listen to me. That's what you'd do,"* Esmeralda says, interrupting my peace.

*"Not now, Esmeralda,"* I think back. This broad is getting bolder by the day. The next time I'm in the spirit room I'll have to figure out a way to keep her invasions in check. There are no bracelets to control her mental comings and goings since she's not a part of my lineage.

"Jayd, did you feel that?" Netta asks, running her fingers through my head.

"Feel what?" Oh hell. The last thing I need is for her to catch wind of Esmeralda's impromptu spirit lessons from beyond the grave.

"It felt like there was an electric shock in your head. It was brief, but it was definitely there." Netta continues to pour the cool water over my hair, repeating the customary Yoruba prayers we say to open and cool the road ahead.

*"Omi tutu, ona tutu, ile tutu, tutu Laroye,"* Esmeralda says, in unison with Netta. *"She's not the only one who can pray, you know."*

Netta jumps back from the impact of Esmeralda's undeniable presence. "There it was again, Jayd. Tell me you didn't feel it that time."

"It's just my ashe, Netta," I say jokingly, but she's not laughing.

"Jayd, as long as I've been washing heads don't you think I can tell the difference between someone's ashe and something else? Don't insult my intelligence, girl."

"It's nothing that I can't handle."

Netta cautiously returns her hands to my head. She's saying prayers in Portuguese now, ones that I've never heard before.

*"She's going to chill your mind out to the point that you're completely relaxed,"* Esmeralda warns. *"By the time your head is cleansed, you'll end up telling her everything she wants to know and more."*

Netta absorbs the electric shock and allows it to fully penetrate her hands. She spreads the energy throughout my scalp, completely coating my head with the cool feeling.

"I'm going to ask you again, Jayd. What is this new vibe I'm feeling, or should I say, who?"

My first instinct is to resist the temptation to tell her the truth about my link with our diabolic neighbor. The more she massages, the more I want to tell her the whole story, right down to the part where Esmeralda told me that she, not Netta, should've been me and my mom's godmother. I love her too much to want to hurt her like that, but she's making it difficulty for me to keep quiet for much longer.

*"Don't hold your tongue, Jayd. It's bad for your health,"* Esmeralda *says, her voice more forceful than before. "The truth shall set you free!"*

The cool vibrations of Esmeralda's ashe course through my forehead and makes its way between my temples. Netta attempts to push the energy back through my head, but it's a battle she can't win. I force Esmeralda's site up to my third eye, rendering Netta's skills mute. She relinquishes her grip on my scalp, disappointed.

"Did you just use your powers against me, little queen?" Netta leans up against the sink, weak from the confrontation.

"I didn't mean to, Netta." I lift my saturated hair out of the sink and sit up straight in my chair. "There are just some things I'm not ready to share with you. I need some space to figure things out for myself first."

"You're not alone, Jayd. You know that, right? Just because Lynn Mae has gone off the deep end doesn't mean that you don't have guidance. That's what I'm here for."

"And I appreciate that. This time, though, I think I'm supposed to do things alone."

"Oh Jayd, you're growing up so fast," Netta says. She tries to hold back her tears but they defy her attempts. "One day I'll look up and you'll be a grown woman, just like I did with your mother."

"I'm not ready to be a grown woman yet." The towel around my shoulders is soaked. Noticing me shiver, Netta hands me a dry towel for my body and another one for my hair.

"Adulthood comes whether you're ready or not. It's best to be ready for the unexpected. And if that means that you have to do your own thing for a while, then as your godmother who loves you, I have to step aside and trust your process. I will always be here to help you when and if you need it."

"Thank you."

Netta bends over the chair and hugs me tightly. She smells like vanilla and ginger, causing me to feel happy despite the circumstances. She's such a blessing. I love all of my mothers, including the ones that act crazy from time to time. I guess we all have the potential to trip. Some of us just do it harder than others.

By the time I got back to Mama's last night, I was too wiped out to finish Jeremy's mojo sack. Esmeralda was relentless with her mental pestering to the point that I had to beg her to let me get some sleep. I don't know if she's lonely in the afterlife or what, but the chick needs to get a life—or death—and leave me be. My attention span is very short this morning due to my zombie state of mind, and so is my patience.

I'm bored out of my mind with Mrs. Bennett's poetry discussion, so much so that I started daydreaming about a life with Chase minus his amnesia. She said that we have twenty minutes to construct a narrative poem about love lost, struggles, or any other common theme within the human experience. I chose to write about it all.

"That's time, class. Any willing volunteers eager to read their work?" Mrs. Bennett catches my eyes. Like Netta, I think she can sense Esmeralda's presence if for no other reason than she was one of Esmeralda's best clients on the low. "Miss Jackson. Why don't you be the first to grace us with your genius?"

Why does she insist on setting me off? I swear this woman is the bane of my existence. Rather than argue what I know will eventually be a losing battle, I choose to oblige her bitchy request.

"An Ode to SNAP," I begin. At the conclusion of the poem, the class looks confused and impressed.

"What is this SNAP thing?" Mrs. Bennett asks, disgusted by the acronym.

The fact that none of my classmates jump in to define the card needed to retrieve monthly aid speaks volumes about the difference between my reality and everyone else's.

"The short version is, it's food stamps."

"If I were you I'd take that out of your poem," she says, without consideration. "Not many people know what that is. It's unnecessary and trite at best."

"Eventhough it's central to the narrative?" Usually I could give a damn about her opinion or her request to edit mine, but this is personal. How dare she judge my poetry?

"Maybe she's not writing for all people to understand her, but for the people in her community to understand her words." Alia thinks she's helping but she's not.

I'm so over arguing with jealous broads like Cameron and even Alia. She hates without even knowing that she's doing it, which is why she's always playing the innocent victim role. It's so played.

"No. People everywhere understand how to use a gift card for store credit, and I'm using food stamps in the same way."

"Well, most people in the general public wouldn't understand that." Alia's tripping. Has she ever listened to NPR?

"It must be nice to be sheltered from the poverty the rest of the country feels on a regular basis." I never thought I'd see the day that I wanted to shake the shit out of Alia, but it's here. And with Esmeralda fresh out of my head I'm liable to do just that.

"The rest of the country isn't poor, Jayd. Maybe that's just your reality," Cameron, says, adding her four cents. "My dad's books talk about how prosperity is all in a person's mind, and that they create their reality. If an entire community, or group of people, is impoverished, then there's something innately dysfunctional in the mindset of those people."

Here we go with her dad's neo-psycho bull.

"Agreed," Mrs. Bennett says, walking toward the white board. She writes down the name of one of Cameron's dad's books, as if we don't already know who the famous psychologist is.

I'm surprised that the books haven't been assigned as mandatory reading as much as Cameron kisses up to our English teacher, not that I'd waste my time reading the garbage. I remember seeing a few of his books on her shelf when I fought her ass over me and Mama's voodoo dolls she got by way of Esmeralda. I should've clocked Cameron's ass over the head with one of his hardcovers. Maybe it would've knocked some sense into her.

"That's one of the most classist, and dare I say racist, things I've ever heard, and y'all have said some real crazy stuff over the years that I've known you."

The entire class falls silent as Mrs. Bennett turns and faces me, like I'm the only one out of order. I own my rude behavior. Maybe she should check her lackey for insensitivity. Before she can figure out a witty comeback, Jeremy steps in.

"So, every population in the world is responsible for their own poverty? Even in an obviously racist and classist caste system like India? Seriously, that's your dad's logic?"

His wifey doesn't look amused at his rationale, but that's one of the things that most attracted me to my ex. Jeremy's nothing if not an intelligent thinking dude.

"I don't know about over there, but over here, in the land of opportunity, there should be no poverty. That's all I'm trying to say."

"Well, keep trying, but it'll never be true," I say. "This country is not the land of opportunity for everyone, only the people it was initially built for. Everyone else has to work ten times as hard to get a piece of the pie, and that pie is usually first bought with food stamps."

Jeremy can't help but chuckle at me bringing the point home. I miss our witty banter, as well as the rest of our relationship when it was good. Too bad I've started to slowly lose respect for him.

"That's enough, Miss Jackson," Mrs. Bennett says, less than pleased with my reasoning. She knows I'm right.

*"Right is relative, chile,"* Esmeralda says.

Mrs. Bennett catches my eye and Esmeralda's familiar chill again, I think.

"Jayd, please see me after class."

Shit. I can't say no to her without suffering some sort of repercussion. I'll be damned if I let this woman question me about her former spiritual advisor.

"May we have another volunteer, please?" Thankfully Mrs. Bennett moves onto another victim.

One of Cameron's followers raises her hand and walks to the center of the room. Finally the attention can turn onto someone else's work.

"Tell me the truth," Jeremy whispers. "Was I the dude in that poem? He sounded familiar."

I can't tell him or anyone else that the guy in the poem was Chase. "It was fiction, Jeremy. Poetry is creative writing, get it?"

"Yeah, but we both know that all fiction is based off of reality, right?"

He does have a point, but in this case, fiction is simply fiction.

*"Don't sell yourself short, Jayd. You don't know what the Creator has in*
*store for you."*
*-Mom*
*Drama High, volume 14: So, So, Hood*

## ~10~
# ROGUE

Fortunately I was able to sneak out of class before Mrs. Bennett or
Jeremy noticed my absence. I'm too drained to deal with either of them
on a one-on-one basis. Jeremy's mojo bag is back on the ancestor
shrine until further notice. Me not being able to finish the final act to
complete the ritual set me back on his work. And him harassing me
about it daily isn't helping his case.

"Hey, Jayd-dizzle," Chase says, falling into to step with me in the
breezeway. No matter how hurt I am, he always makes me smile. "Got a
little proposal for you."

"It better not have anything to do with Jeremy because the
answer's no," I say, quickening my pace. I don't want to be late to fourth
period. "I already told him to get in line. He's not the only one who
needs help these days."

"Easy, Jayd. E-weezy," he says, mimicking one of our favorite
characters from *Be Cool*. We must've watched that movie a hundred
times last summer. "No girl, nothing like that." Chase steps in front of
my classroom door. "Unfortunately, my betrothed's health has taken a

turn for the worst. She's got a full-blown case of the flu."

"And you want me to go with you to bring her soup again?" I say, sarcastically. This dude is whipped on the wrong chick and I can't do a damn thing about it.

"*Or can you?*" Esmeralda says, invading my thoughts.

"*Bye, Esmeralda,*" I think back. Surprisingly, she disappears for the moment. If I knew it was that easy to get rid of her I would've done that a long time ago rather than entertaining her crazy ass.

"Nah, shawty. Actually, we planned an impromptu college tour down south and she can't go. Thought you might want to take her place. It's fully paid for, and since my grandpa's an alum, they're going to show this prospective student a good time."

"I thought you had your heart set on Morehouse?"

"I do, but that doesn't mean I can't check out other schools. Besides, it's in your hometown. Thought you'd appreciate the trip."

"My hometown is Compton, my brotha."

He steps to the side and allows other students inside. Apparently, Chase isn't concerned with being tardy to his next class. "Okay, then your ancestral hometown."

"New Orleans?" The hairs on the back of my neck stand at attention. What are the chances that I'd get a free trip to NOLA?

145

"The one and only. So, you down or what?"

"I have to clear it with my mom, but yeah. I'm down." Hell yeah, I'm going. Something tells me that it's right where I need to be to effectively handle my business.

"Cool. We'll have a good time," Chase says, walking backwards. "And besides, Alia trusts me to be with you, no one else. Let's do it big in NOLA, girl."

Alia should probably think twice about trusting me.

"Sounds like a plan."

"Good shit. The plane leaves at six Friday evening. My mom's going to be ecstatic that you're coming. We'll fly out of New Orleans Sunday morning. Good times, baby girl. Good times."

"Sounds like a full weekend. I'm looking forward to it."

The bell rings loudly overhead. Chase sprints toward his class and I step fully into mine.

Shit, I forgot that I told Summer I'd work under her this weekend. I know she's done giving me passes, and frankly, I'm done taking them. I really don't want to work for her or anyone other than Mama and Netta. Hell, in all honestly, I'm about ready to stop that, too, and focus more on my own business.

*"That sounds like a queen who's ready to finally claim her crown,"*

146

Esmeralda says, again speaking directly into my thoughts.

*"Why do you keep doing that?"* I think back, annoyed. Her voice in my head is getting old.

*"I'm not doing it. You are."*

*"No, Esmeralda. I'm pretty sure that you're infiltrating my head, and I don't appreciate it at all, especially not while I'm in class."*

The teacher puts the daily prompt on the board as the class quietly evaluates the question. I take out my notebook and attempt to focus on the task at hand.

Esmeralda continues with her interruption. *"Think about it, Jayd. How else could I be here when you're awake? Your mother was able to do the same thing, only when you came into your power. Don't you get it by now? It stems from you, not us."*

*"In the last dream that I had about my mom I felt like I woke up with her sight but I didn't have it,"* I say, recalling the powerful vision.

*"That's because you thought her only power was the one she has innately, not the one she gained as your mother, which you also have access to."*

*"I see."* I guess you do learn something new every day, even if it is via our immortal enemy.

*"Not yet, but you will if you let go and trust yourself to develop*

*accordingly.*"

"*What's that supposed to mean?*"

"*It means that you're still acting like an apprentice when you need to be working like a priestess. The only way that the work is going to get done is if you do it, little queen.*"

"*My grandmother's the queen, not me.*" Why do I have to keep reminding people of this?

"*Ha! Not anymore. She gave that crown away when she let your grandfather into the spirit room, and you know that. Have you been in there lately?*"

Actually, no, but that's not her business.

"*Esmeralda, all I need to know is how to send that canine lover of yours back to wherever the hell you got him from. I'm sure you two have a lot of catching up to do.*" I wish she'd shut up so that I can focus on my work.

"*Stop evading the subject, child. Heed my advice. The only way you're going to succeed is to let go of your childish ways, Jayd. You must go rogue and rugged with your talents. Good or bad, you can't be afraid of your powers, sleep or awake.*"

"*Right now I'm more worried about your untamed household. What the hell, Esmeralda?*"

*"As you said. He's on his own. I have no power to control anything he does from this realm. Only your grandmother can do that now, unless..."*

I guess Rousseau wasn't lying, but obviously Esmeralda knows more than he does.

*"Unless what?"*

*"You can do more than borrow powers through your dreams, young queen,"* Esmeralda snarls. *"You can become the object of your possession—just for a little while, but long enough to walk in their shoes, literally."*

*"Are you saying that if I snatch your powers in my dreams I can also take your place in reality?"*

*"Something like that, yes. Your mother's a good example. Just like other people in your dreams, you can also become those subjects when you wake up."*

*"And where are they in the meantime?"*

*"Here somewhere, with the rest of us, I suppose."*

*"How much time would I have in the other person's shoes?"*

*"No telling, just like dreaming. It ends when it ends. You'll have to finally surrender to your powers, Jayd. That's what being a queen is truly about. Trusting yourself and the power that lies within. Your mother fought*

*it, denied it, and ultimately lost it. Your grandmother's suppressing it yet*

*again for her man. Now it's your turn. What ever will you do with your*

*crown?"*

"*You're enjoying this, aren't you?*" I shake my head at my options.

If only I could simply worry about schoolwork and boys for a change.

"*Oh, very much so. I could've seen this coming a mile away. Love is*

*the kryptonite of the Williams' legacy. It kills y'all every time. All I have to*

*do is sit back and watch it unfold.*"

"*You're done.*" And again, just like that she's gone.

I consider all that I just learned. It's a bit overwhelming. Mama

and I aren't on the best of terms, but there's still work to do. I need her

help with figuring all of this shit out whether she wants to assist or not.

Like Chase, I am getting excited about our trip down south this

weekend.


I want to talk to Mama about that and the work we need to get

done, as well as everything Esmeralda dropped on me earlier. To my

surprise she's in the spirit room-turned-love shack alone this afternoon.

Even if it is Mama's private house under construction, the shrines are

still in tact and that's all that matters. Putting everything back in order

after our last encounter was therapeutic in a way. Hopefully she's feeling the love for me today rather than still being pissed.

"Mama, would you please focus on the task at hand," I plead. She's getting on my last nerve, acting more like Mickey than my grandmother. "I need your help to get rid of Rousseau and his band of strays. They're not going to stop unless we stop them."

"Jayd, we don't have to do anything. They'll eventually get hit by a car or picked up by animal control. And Rousseau always goes astray without his owner to keep him on a tight leash, which is exactly what I'm doing with my man," she says, a little more coquettish than necessary. "So no, I can't help you with this because frankly my dear, I don't give a damn."

Mama laughs at her own wit but I don't find it funny. I hated watching *Gone with the Wind* when I was a child, and don't appreciate the reference now.

"Mama, you know you're wrong for this." I take Jeremy's mojo bag off of the ancestor shrine and tuck it safely away in my bra. Mama taught me that trick when I was ten years old. Close to my heart is the best place to put important things.

"Girl, please. I keep telling you that you'll learn one day. If the Creator continues to bless you with a long, healthy life, you'll live long enough to see what I'm talking about." Mama passes me by to enter the kitchen.

"I don't have that kind of time."

"You better pray that you do, little girl."

Instead of arguing with my grandmother, I decide to let her have this one. One of us has to focus on the mission at hand rather than the moment. I claim a few more items from the shrine and head for the door where Lexi's lounging, as usual. It'll be nice to do my spirit work in New Orleans. I have a feeling that my efforts will be more powerful with the ashe of my ancestors instantly attainable.

"Jayd, what are you up to?"

"Nothing more than you already know about, Mama. I have homework to finish."

"I've known you all of your life and more, Jayd. Don't lie to me. You know that it won't end well for you if you try."

Mama looks at me like she wants to probe my mind but stops short of doing it. Maybe she knows that I know my powers extend past simple dreaming. If she does, she wouldn't have told me, just like she won't tell me now. Some things I have to learn as I go, but unfortunately when it comes to the hellhound next door I don't have the luxury of time to grow up. I have to figure out how to stop Rousseau immediately before we run out of time, with or without Mama's help.

"I would never attempt to hide anything from you, Mama. Besides, I'm not the one trying to keep the other in the dark."

"Watch yourself, Jayd. You've been getting a little too sassy for my liking." Mama's green eyes glow with anger. She focuses her vision on mine and makes sure to lock onto my site. Unfortunately for her I've started to master the art of disabling other powers before they can affect my own. If she were on her game she'd know that by now.

"I never mean you any disrespect, Mama. I hope you know that." My brown eyes begin to take on a glow of their own, and again, Mama chooses not to continue her probing.

"Actions speak so much louder than words ever will, Jayd. And right now all of your actions say that you are challenging my authority, and that can only end badly for you."

"In a perfect world, you'd never feel that way about me because you would know that I've always respected your status. It's you who has seem to forgotten your crown lately in order to please your husband, and that's truly unfortunate. I love you, Mama. Good night."

*"After the bitter always comes the sweet. Have faith in the sweet, Jayd. Hold out for the sweet."*
*–Mama*
*Drama High, volume 17: Sweet Dreams*

## ~11~
# A PERFECT WORLD

*It's a hot, muggy evening. My husband's dinner is on the stove, and there are three children catching fire flies on the back porch. The glass mason jars twinkle in the dark with the bright insects dancing inside. The children giggle with excitement as a car pulls into the driveway.*

*"Just in time. It smells delicious in here," he says, opening the front screen door. It's Rah. He's here in the dream with me again. As usual, he's loving every moment of our shared experience.*

*"What are you doing here?" I ask, turning away from the stove, shocked to see him in my kitchen.*

*"What are you talking about? I live here. Baby, are you feeling okay?"*

*I step back and block his advance. Something's definitely not right with this situation.*

"Babe, I didn't know what kind of greens you wanted tonight, so I got both collards and kale," Chase says, stepping into the kitchen from the living room entrance.

Rah looks from me to Chase, disturbed. "What the hell, Jayd?"

Chase sets the groceries on the kitchen table and walks over to where I'm standing. He kisses me on the lips and rubs my stomach. "Rah, what's up, man? Are you joining me and the Mrs. for dinner?"

Rah, silent, looks at my stomach with the same dazed expression I'm wearing. I'm pregnant, and Chase is my husband?

"Nah, man. I've got to head out." Rah tries to play off his shock, but his anger's still obvious to me. "I just dropped by to see how y'all were doing. I guess everything's good, real good."

"Yeah, man. Why wouldn't it be?" Chase continues to rub my belly. "Third time's a charm, right? Have you and Trish started working on number four yet?"

Again, Rah looks as stunned by the revelation as I am. "Not that I know of, man."

"Well, surprises happen, my brotha. And it's all good." Chase takes me in his arms and hugs me tightly. He smells as good as always. This

155

feels so natural and right, even with Rah's death stare searing holes into both my eyes.

I shut my eyes closed to avoid the burning sensation. What the hell?

"I'll let you two get back to your evening. It was nice catching up." Rah turns to exit through the back door.

"Yeah, man. Anytime. Don't be a stranger," Chase says, letting me go and focusing on the cooking pots on the stove.

"Seems as if I already am," Rah says, barely audible, but I heard him loud and clear. He glances up at me one final time, shooting the same heated look and this time, it's unavoidable.

"Ahhhh." I groan from the discomfort before falling to the floor.

"Jayd!" Chase screams, falling to the floor next to me. "Is it the baby?"

"No. My head." I rub my temples to alleviate the pain but it's no use. The throbbing in my head gets louder with every breath that I take.

Chase looks at Rah who's still standing in the doorway. "Rah, call 911."

*Rah doesn't respond. Instead, he stares on motionless and doesn't release his gaze.*

*"Rah, did you hear me?" Chase yells. "Call an ambulance. We have to get Jayd some help."*

*"You're her husband. You got this, right?"*

*Chase looks like he wants to punch the shit out of Rah but instead, reaches into his back pocket for his cell. Rah turns away from my pain, walks down the porch steps and pass the children toward his car. No matter how mad he ever got at me, the Rah I know would never leave me crippled on the floor in pain.*

My phone rings. Thank God for the intrusion. I think Rah just figured out my little secret. Oh well. I can't cry over spilled milk, no matter how sour it is.

"Hello," I speak into my cell.

"Jayd. I need help and I don't know who else to call," Mickey says, frantically.

"Where are you?" I kick the covers off of my body and let the cool morning air fully wake me up, glad to be out of the disturbing shared dream with Rah. Usually our dreams are more erotic. I don't know why the mood turned violent, but I'm sure I'll hear from him about it at some point.

"I'm caught up in Fresno. Can you believe that bitch's mama actually had me arrested for kidnapping my own baby? My own daughter!"

"I guess that bitch you're referring to would be Nigel?"

Mickey's not amused by my feigned ignorance. "Hell yeah that's the bitch I'm referring to," she says, cynically. "Can you help me out of this shit or not?"

"What do you want me to do, Mickey? You need a lawyer, not a friend."

Unfortunately, my school outfit hanging on the back of the bedroom door needs to be ironed. Between that, the joint dream with Rah, and Mickey's voice first thing, this day is already off to a bad start.

"No I need a magician, and you're the closest thing that I've got to one."

That comparison doesn't sit well with me. "I'm not a magician, Mickey. My family's legacy isn't a trick or some sort of circus show. This shit is real, and more often than not it also comes with its share of pain."

Quite honestly, I'm tired of helping my friends get out of their own self-created bull at my own risk.

"Jayd, please. You know you love this shit," Mickey says, indifferently. "I need you to whip up some of those stay-out-of-jail goodies you made for the white boy."

"The white boy has a name, and furthermore, I'm not your personal chef," I say, done with Mickey's spoiled attitude.

"Damn, Jayd. I wish Esmeralda were still alive. At least she helped people whenever they asked, no judgment included."

"She helped people because they were her clients, not out of loyalty or friendship. You haven't offered to pay me even a compliment for helping your ungrateful ass and I'm over it. I don't owe you a thing."

"What's got your panties in a bunch this morning?"

"Friends and they're expectations, that's what."

"I'm sorry I called you, Jayd. I thought as Nickey's godmother that you'd help her mama out, but I guess I was wrong. As a matter of, fact, I don't even want you to be her godmother anymore. Consider yourself fired."

"I don't think that's your call anymore. Good luck with getting out." I press end on the call. My blood's boiling I'm so hot.

*"Watch it, little girl. You're getting more and more like your real godmother everyday,"* Esmeralda says, pleased.

*"Please don't start with me, not today."* All the pleading in the world won't stop Esmeralda from running her mental mouth, but it's still worth a shot.

*"Poor thing. By your age I had enough men to keep my stress down. Seems you need a little love and affection to make you feel better, no?"*

*"Mind your business, Esmeralda."* I hate to admit it, but she does have a point.

*"What do you think I'm doing? You are my business."*

*"Bye, bye."* I can't press end but I can hang up on her in my own way.

Esmeralda leaves just as quickly as she appeared, and I am grateful for the few moments of peace before my day really begins. I claim my toiletry bag from the nightstand and head to the bathroom before I lose my opportunity to get in. My bags are already packed for my New Orleans escapade. I can't get out of here fast enough.

I can't remember the last time I was so excited about a Friday morning. I'm actually looking forward to going to school today just to get it over with. Chase is going to take me to my mom's apartment afterschool so that I can finish packing and officially get her permission to attend the festivities at the college. I have to have an adult's signature, and Mama's not the one to ask at the moment.

"Jayd," Rah says, slowing his car down ahead of me. Shit. I don't have time for his drama this morning. "Get in, please."

Honestly, I'm not mad at getting a ride to school. I've got to get my mom's car fixed or save up for another vehicle of my own. Taking the bus has officially gotten old.

"What the hell was that dream about last night? I can't shake it."

Me neither, but he doesn't need to know that. "It was just a dream, Rah. And don't worry, as soon as I have a moment I'm going to figure out how to stop sharing them with you."

"All of our dreams have had a little truth in them. You want to tell me why you were knocked up by Chase in this one?" Rah asks, heading toward the seven-ten freeway. Hopefully there's not too much traffic this morning. I can't take a full-blown interrogation.

"Who knows, Rah?"

"I think you do."

Drake interrupts our tense conversation, mellowing us both out. I love this song.

"That chick in *Hotline Bling* sounds like she went wild after Drake. Not a good look for a queen, you feel me?"

"So let me get this straight. A dude can go off, make a name for himself without being attached to a girl. As a matter of fact, being unattached to many girls at the same time, and that's ok? But when she picks herself up, gets a new crew, shines in the darkness that he left behind to the point where he almost doesn't recognize her and she no longer needs his ass, then she's a hoe?"

"Don't get me wrong. I'm not mad at a shorty for getting hers. She just needs to have some self respect while doing it. No chick wants to become a THOT."

"A powerful female instantly becomes one of 'them hoes out there' when she stops messing with a dude and starts getting hers? Really, Rah?"

"No need to get mad at the truth or me. I didn't make the rules," he says, merging onto the ninety-one freeway. Thank God we're almost to Redondo Beach.

"You didn't but men did, and that's the problem."

"You're tripping hard for no reason, girl. Chill."

"Am I tripping, or are you mad because I'm acting like the chick in *Hotline Bling*? I got my shit together, without you, Rah. For once, one of the girls you've infected with your love and charm and chivalry got up from under your spell, and it pisses you off."

Rah's silent for a few minutes as we continue our ride toward the beach. Part of him wants to admit that I'm telling the truth, but his ego can't handle it.

When we reach a stoplight he turns and faces me. "You're turning into someone that I don't recognize. Hell, I'm not sure I even like this new person."

"Sounds like a personal problem to me."

"Whatever, Jayd. You can act tough all you want, but I know you, the real you. This little tough girl act you've got going on ain't you."

"It's not an act," I say, pointing at the green light. We continue our drive in silence. The closer we get to South Bay High the thicker the traffic becomes, giving us too much time to sulk.

"You gave it up to that rich, white boy, didn't you?" Rah finally says, referring to Jeremy the same way Mickey did this morning. "Damn, Jayd. I thought you were better than that."

"What the hell is that supposed to mean?"

"It means that I never knew your cookies were for sale."

"You did not just say that to me. Seriously, Rah? Seriously? Have you met your baby mama?"

"No need to bring Sandy into this but since you did, that's exactly my point. I always thought you were saving yourself for someone special. At least someone better than Jeremy's punk ass."

Rah's jealousy is filing the car it's so thick.

"Who? Like you?" I ask, staring at the right side of Rah's face. His chiseled cheekbone tenses up as his grip on the steering wheel tightens.

164

"Yes, like me, or at the very least not Jeremy. He doesn't deserve you."

"No, he doesn't." Finally, we agree on something this morning. "And neither do you."

"Whatever, Jayd. Like I said, you're not acting like yourself lately, and I'm done trying to reason with you."

"How come I'm not allowed to shake shit up every once in a while without being judged for it?" I don't need anyone's permission to be me. It's about time that everyone recognized that."

"Shake shit up? What the hell for, Jayd? You're perfectly fine the way that you are, or were." Rah opens the passenger's visor and flips open the attached mirror. "I don't know who this chick is, and I'm not sure I want to."

He stops at the intersection before the main cross street to campus. The traffic is still locked up, as usual. I can't take another moment stuck in the car with Rah and his hate.

"You know what, Rah? I don't live my life for you or anyone else. If you don't like the fact that I'm over pining after your scary ass then so be it. I'm done." I grab my things and open my door.

"Jayd, sit back down. Are you crazy?"

"No. Quite the opposite. For the first time in a long time I feel completely sane."

I slam the heavy car door and begin my hike up the steep hill. Rah's still calling after me, but the faster I walk the less I can hear his words.

*"Careful with your emotions, Jayd. If they're left unchecked for too long they can overpower your senses."*

"Don't worry, I'm in full control of my head, Esmeralda, but thanks for the warning," I say, aloud.

My breathing gets heavier the further I go. No matter how many times I've walked up this street I never can seem to get used to this hill.

*"Really?"* Esmeralda laughs sinisterly. *"If that were true I wouldn't be here, would I?"*

I refuse to think that I'm loosing my good sense, even if Esmeralda keeps working my last nerve whenever she feels like it.

*"Your grandmother would have you and your mama believe that I just went crazy all on my own, but that's not the case. My rage was sparked by neglect and fueled by jealousy. Without my godfamily to sustain me, or*

*my god sister, I was left out in the cold, and that's what I became: ice cold. Your grandmother has no one to blame for my actions but herself. Lynn Mae was the root cause of all of our drama, her and her coward of a husband."*

"Watch it, Esmeralda. Those are my grandparents you're talking about." I finally reach the top and cross the street. There are students hanging out front before the bell rings in ten minutes.

*"Truth is truth, though, ain't it? And if I'm lying you can shut me up. But you know I'm right, don't you, little queen? In a perfect world, men are to be controlled. If not, they become poison in our lives. Heed my words, child. Don't let these boys rule your head. Rule theirs instead. Don't worry. I know when it's time for me to go."*

With Mama noticeably absent from my head these days, her undead nemesis's words are starting to make more sense every day. Why is it so easy to give up my power to a dude, or my mom and grandmother to do the same thing when they choose to do so? We've never been considered weak women, however, when it comes to the men that we truly love there seems to be a choice to be made: love or power. She's right. In a perfect world there would be more of a balance that benefited women in love. For the Williams women, it seems that the balance will never be achieved as long as we want to maintain our power. Maybe it really is up to me to bring some balance back to our lineage, and the trip to New Orleans this evening is the perfect way to begin to strike that balance for us all.

*"It's hard for Mama to understand why everyone can't be as strong as she is"*
*- Jayd*
*Drama High, volume 12: Pushin'*

## ~12~
# SHE'S BACK

As luck would have it, there was a substitute teacher for Mrs. Bennett today, and I couldn't have been more grateful. Me not having to deal with her overly curious probing is a blessing. That's all I needed to get my mind right for our flight in a couple of hours.

Flying isn't as fun as it used to be on my summer trips to Chicago. My mom's cousin would have us out nearly every July for the holiday. But now that planes have so many restrictions that it takes the fun out of travelling by air.

Chase is more excited about the trip than I am, and rightfully so. He's looking forward to spending more time with his birth mother's family, and her dad is the one sponsoring our college visit to his alma mater. I know Chase isn't truly considering Louisiana for college. It's more about spending time getting to his black side than anything else.

Chase is also concerned with Alia's health, who's milking every moment of being under the weather. Chase has been on the phone with her the entire ride to Inglewood in order to reassure her that our trip's

169

strictly about handling his business. As boring as the conversation is, he can't blame me for dozing off until we reach our destination. Besides, I haven't heard from Esmeralda since her visit earlier, which hopefully means that she's taking the rest of the day off. A nap is definitely in order.

*"Dig deeper, Jayd," Maman's voice says from a distance. "I know that it's difficult work, but one of us has got to get it done. Right now you're the only one who can do it."*

*The shovel in my hands rubs me the wrong way. My hands are bleeding from the blisters forming in my palms. The smell of fresh earth keeps me energized to continue digging, as does Maman's constant cheering. I wipe the sweat from my brow with the back of my right hand.*

*"No stopping, Jayd! We haven't a moment to waste. We must get both of them in the ground as soon as possible."*

*"Yes, ma'am."*

*Where is she barking orders from? I can hear her but my great-grandmother's nowhere in sight. I focus my eyes as much as possible in the pervasive darkness and read one of the headstones across the vast lawn. The two small caskets at my feet are familiar. Apparently I'm burying*

*Rousseau and Esmeralda's voodoo dolls in a New Orleans graveyard.*

*Perfect. Perhaps they'll both stay dead this time.*

*"That's good enough." Maman materializes in front of me and points*

*to the large, white tomb straight ahead. "My enemies shall bow at my feet.*

*Make it so."*

*I take the small caskets and place them carefully inside of the large*

*hole in the ground. There are so many questions that I'd like to ask her but*

*I know this isn't the right time for a spirit lesson. For example, there are a*

*few veves that I don't recognize. One of my first lessons early in childhood*

*was to memorize the symbols representative of the various loas and*

*orishas in the voodoo pantheon. As well versed as I am in most things*

*voodoo, some of these figures are completely foreign to me.*

*"Ashes to ashes. Dust to dust. We don't enjoy disabling our*

*enemies, but more often than not it's a must." Maman reaches down into*

*the fresh mound of soil, takes a healthy portion in her smooth palms, and*

*tosses it over both boxes.*

*"Will this ultimately kill them once and for all?"*

*"People with ashe are never truly dead. They're crossed over, and if*

*peaceful, they mostly leave the living alone. That is our goal with*

Esmeralda and Rousseau. We want them to leave the living be, and focus on being better ancestors to the people who want to call upon their ashe."

"But what if they don't want to be better? What if they want to be as evil in the afterlife as they were in this life?"

"You can't worry about the outcome, Jayd. Focus on the work and it will all unfold as it's intended to." Maman taps on her naked wrist as an indication that time is of the essence.

"I get it, Maman. I hear you, loud and clear." I pick up a large pile of soil with the shovel and continue to bury Esmeralda and her man-pet, Rousseau.

"Good. You're going to have to be strong to submerge these two. They don't die quickly or quietly. That's why the job must be done properly and completely, at my feet. Do you understand, child?"

"Yes, I understand. It'll be done properly, trust that." Each shovel full of dirt becomes heavier and heavier but I keep going, spreading it as evenly as I possibly can. The salt of my sweat makes its way in between my lips eventhough it's cold outside.

*"We are trusting you, young one. This is a very important time in the survival of our lineage. Be sure that you're up to the work, Jayd. Heavy is the head that wears our crown, young woman. The neck must be strong."*

"Jayd, wake up. We're here," Chase says, turning off the engine.

I shake myself up and look around. The smell of wet soil is still fresh in my nose. If that wasn't a direct message from my great-grandmother, I don't know what is. Luckily, I packed the spirit book as well as other essential tools for the trip. There's always work to be done no matter the zip code.

"I'm going to call my girl back while you get your stuff," Chase says, his cell already in hand. "Tell your mom I said hey."

"Okay. I won't be long." Chase is such a good boyfriend. I hope Alia treats him better this time around. If she takes advantage of him in any way she'll have hell to pay.

I jog up the steps and unlock the door. "Hey, mom."

"Hey, baby. How are you?" she asks, walking out of the dining room and kissing me on the cheek.

"Good. Just rushing. Chase is waiting for me downstairs and told me to tell you hi."

"Chase, huh?" she asks. She also remembers our brief relationship and how hurt I was when I had to give it up. "How's he doing?"

"He's good. Rushing like me."

"Why are you both in such a hurry?"

"We're going on a college tour in New Orleans," I say, passing her the paperwork and quickly packing a few more things into my bag. It's difficult living between two spaces. I always forget something in one place or another. "Chase's girl got sick at the last minute and I get to take her place."

"Why is this the first I'm hearing about it?" my mom asks, quickly glancing over the college permission slip and first class ticket attached. "And why didn't you ask Mama to go?"

"I'm sorry for the late request, really, I am. Chase just asked me a couple of days ago and honestly I wasn't sure how I would feel about going with him at first." She doesn't need to know about the dream I had in the graveyard, or that Esmeralda's my current spiritual advisor, whether I want her to be or not. "And you know that Mama could care less about what I do these days. Please, mom. It's important."

My mom shakes her head and sighs deeply. "You still should tell Mama about this." She signs the document and hands it back to me. "Have fun, baby, and be good. You do know that no matter what state Mama's in at the moment, she's not letting you go away to college."

"I don't know if Mama's thinking about anything but her and Daddy at the moment." I fold the paper in half and place it in my purse. Hopefully I have everything I need for the weekend.

"Trust me, Jayd. You moving outside of Los Angeles County to attend college isn't an option no matter how distracted my mother's right now." My mom hugs me tightly and kisses my forehead. "You moving far away by yourself would wake her up in more ways than one. Never doubt her love for you. Ever."

If that's the case, then maybe this trip will be enough to shake some sense into Mama after all. "Thank you, mom. I'll call you when we land."

"Okay, young woman. And tell Chase to take care of my baby."

The flight was so comfortable and quicker than I anticipated. I've never travelled in style before and I'm loving it. Alia's missing out and

I'm so glad that I'm here instead. New Orleans smells and feels like home. I can't believe I'm finally here, and with Chase no less.

"Our chariot awaits," Chase says, ushering me toward the black Escalade with a driver included.

"Remind me to always travel with you."

"Sounds like a plan, Miss Jackson." Chase takes my hand and helps me step up into the truck while he and the driver take care of our bags.

"Thanks, Ivan," Chase says as he closes the door.

Once we're all inside, Ivan heads to the five-star hotel his mother also set up for us. Mrs. Carmichael was happy that me and her son were finally together, something she always wanted and was never shy about letting us know. I love her, too, and wish I could be back in their house again. I almost forgot how good they treated me.

"I set up a few meetings at the college all day tomorrow and figured you could tour the city, unless you want to look around the school, too."

"Nah, I'm good. I have work to do and would love to sight see," starting with my great-grandmother's infamous tomb.

"I got you," Chase says, handing me three hundred dollar bills. "This should hold you until tomorrow night. And everything's comped at the hotel. Just charge it to the room."

"Chase, I can't take your money. The trip is already enough." I attempt to press the folded bills into his hands but he's not having it.

"Hey, you're subbing for my girl this weekend, right? Therefor, you get treated like my girl, minus the kinky shit, of course," he says, laughing.

That's the shit I miss the most, not his constant spoiling, even if it's also lovely. "Thank you, Chase."

"That's more like it. And, you're very welcome. Now, about tonight," he says, clapping his hands excitedly. "We've got a couple of party invites, including one from my grandpa's fraternity. You down?"

"I don't know, Chase. I'm a bit tired. Can I get a nap in first and then we'll see?"

"Of course, girl. We'll drop you off," Chase says, pointing at the Omni hotel in the heart of the French Quarter. "You can get settled and text me later if you're up to it. I'll send the car back for you."

"Thank you. It's been a long week."

"I feel you. Promise me you'll have some fun this weekend," Chase says, pointing at the stash in my hand. "You can't work the entire time. We're in NOLA, baby. You gotta let loose a little bit."

"You're right. I promise I'll have some fun."

"Good shit, Lady J."

The driver pulls up to the hotel and parks the truck. "Mr. Carmichael, sir."

"Thanks, man. Come on, Jayd. Let's get checked in and then I'll leave you be."

After a quick nap, I showered and changed clothes before hitting the streets. Other than the cat-sized rats, New Orleans is a lovely city. It's after midnight and Chase is just getting started with his party hopping. I checked in with him a little while ago and he's having a ball.

I've walked through the French Court over to the Tremé side of town where I stood a while in Congo Square soaking up my ancestors' ashe. Afterwards, I had a large bowl of some of the best gumbo ever, and then two beignets and a café au lait from Café du Monde. So far, this has been the best trip ever.

*"You do realize that you're not a tourist,"* Maman says, interrupting my peaceful night.

*"Yes, Maman,"* I think back. *"However, technically speaking, I've never been here before, so tonight I'm going to do the tourist thing."*

*"You haven't seen the most important tourist attraction yet. Follow me."* Maman materializes before my eyes. She's not completely in her physical form, but more animated then I've ever seen her before.

"How did you do that?" I ask, in complete awe of Maman's transformation. It's amazing all of the secrets that my lineage has yet to reveal.

"This is my city, Jayd. Here I am quite alive," she says, leading me down Canal Street. "Here," she says, pressing money into my right palm. "Throw these coins at the crossroads for Legba."

There's a perfectly balanced intersection straight ahead. I say a quick prayer to our father orisha to open our path for success.

"Alright, child. Let's move," Maman says. She moves quickly up the street not sparing a second.

The streets are filled with happy people, mostly tourists like myself. Maman moves easily through the crowds. Her tignon is hidden by a sheer veil that covers her entire head.

"I can see why there are still reports of your sightings."

Maman smiles and nods her head in acknowledgment. "Precisely, my dear." Her emerald eyes twinkle under the dim street lamps.

We continue walking for a few moments more. Maman turns onto Basin Street where we approach the gate of Saint Louis Cemetery number one. This is where her well-adored tomb stands in her husband's family plot. Til death do them part.

"Come, child. Let's get to work." Maman turns her back to the gate, crosses herself three times, and directs me to do the same before we enter. This wasn't a part of my dream.

"Careful not to disturb the other burial sites here, love. We don't want to awaken the wrong spirits."

"Will do."

Maman kisses her fingers as she passes certain graves. "We are going to dig up some of the soil near my tomb for you to take home so that you can properly bury Rousseau and Esmeralda once and for all."

"But how? We already buried Esmeralda's doll, and I don't have one for Rousseau."

"I'm going to give you what you need to create their dolls for this ritual. Don't worry. I know what I'm doing."

"I don't doubt that, but Rousseau's been missing in action lately. I'm not even sure he's still alive."

"Jayd, sweetie. That dog has more than one trick up his sleeve. You should know better than to underestimate your enemies by now...all of them."

"I thought he could only control animals?"

"What greater animal is there than an angry young man or any woman for that matter? How do you think he and Esmeralda hooked up in the first place? Like attracts like, Jayd. And the two of them are more alike than not. As long as he lives, she lives."

Well, damn. I never thought of it like that. Has she been playing me this entire time?

"Yes, she has," Maman says, catching my thought just like her daughter does when she's on her game. "Ego is the biggest toy that there is, but no need to worry about that now. It's in the past. You, my

181

dear, must focus on the present. And in this moment, you need to figure out how to save my daughter from herself, and that means getting your shit together."

Real talk. Maman is more than pissed if she's cussing at me.

"And how exactly do I do that?" I look around the graveyard and notice flashlights in the distance. Ever since they've made Maman's tomb a paid tourist attraction, security has been deep in the cemetery. They tried to blame it on voodoo and tourists, but the Laveau name will always attract money—that's one of the main benefits of being Oshune's daughter.

"The first thing you can do is to stop entertaining her. Do not allow her into your head at any time, whether you are awake or dreaming, unless you call her. Even then, don't let her linger."

"I can't do that, Maman. She just pops up when I'm least expecting it."

"Oh, Jayd. My dear, sweet, innocent, and sometimes so very stupid great-granddaughter."

Did she just call me stupid?

"You still doubt your powers, and that is the weakness that Esmeralda exploits the most, her and her legionnaires. The moment that you realize once and for all that it is you and only you who controls your dreams, who enters them, and when, that is when you'll keep our enemies at bay."

Esmeralda alluded to that more than once but I didn't give it much thought.

"She's made some good points, though." I walk around the tomb, eyeing the grandness of it compared to all the others. It's not the biggest or the most expensive, but it is by far the most loved. "Mainly, that I have to honor my dark side like I do its opposite."

Maman meets me in front of her headstone and stops me in my tracks. "Don't we all? But the key in that lesson is not to give in to it, ever. Choose to use the tools in your arsenal very carefully, Jayd.

"How do I keep my powers in check when I can't even fully control them?"

"It's all about balance, baby. Yes, your tongue can be a lethal weapon when you desire, but is it constructive in the long run? Yes, sex is powerful and can be used to break up the strongest of unions, but will that lead to ultimate happiness and joy? There are so many powers at your disposal as a woman on this journey, but I guarantee you that karma is the biggest bitch of them all. Mark my words, Jayd. Not only do you reap what you sow, but you also eat it."

The lights get closer and I know my time is running out. I promised Chase that I'd meet him at the last party, which started over an hour ago. He hasn't texted me in the past couple of hours. I'll take that as a sign that he's enjoying the visit.

"I have to go, Maman. I heard you. Every word. And I promise, I'll do my part to protect our lineage. You have my word."

"I don't want your word, Jayd. I want your power." Maman grabs both of wrists and shakes them. "Fix this shit, child. Once and for all. You have to humble Esmeralda and her brood. There can only be one reigning queen at a time, and she will never be it."

Suddenly I hear dogs in the distance accompanying the staggered lights hurriedly flashing in my direction. I replace my hood and run toward the exit, but it's no use. The dogs are hot on my trail. How does Esmeralda do it?

*"Exactly, Jayd. How does she do it?"* Maman says into my mind. *"Channel her energy like she does yours and use it to save yourself, now!"*

Rather than run from the hungry beasts, I turn around and calmly face them.

"Maman, I'm scared," I whisper. Everything in me says to run. That's what we do where I from when we see dogs. I know PETA might think differently about the furry canines, but I run first, pet later.

"I know, baby. So am I, but you can't let your fear stop you from moving forward. Show these dogs who's boss and keep moving, Jayd. Time is of the essence."

I focus on their growling snarls and sharp teeth glistening under the light of the full moon. Rather than give in to my fear, I think about Esmeralda's eyes in my earlier dream at the graveyard. My head begins to pulsate just like it does when Esmeralda catches my site with her vision. I allow the ice-cold migraine to completely take over my head without managing the pain.

"Ahhh! I can't take anymore, Maman. It's too much."

"In order to possess her power you also have to tolerate the pain. It will hurt, but it doesn't have to rule you." Maman's words fade into the background and so does her physical form as the shepherds' growls become more menacing. I guess they don't like Esmeralda's ice-cold stare any more than I do.

185

Slowly, they cower to the pain of me taking over their heads and I can feel their stomachs' growl. How cruel of Esmeralda and Rousseau to keep animals hungry in order to train them to do their dirty work.

As the security guards gain ground I make my escape through the broken fence and run as fast as I can toward the intersection where I left the offering for Legba. I retrieve the offering and head toward the university campus. My work is done for the night. When I return to California, I will check Esmeralda and her man-dog one last time. I have my work cut out for me. An eye for an eye, a tooth for a tooth. Luckily, I can get both in one shot.

*"But no matter what, I refuse to allow this school to make me forget who I am and where I come from."*
*-Jayd*
*Drama High, volume 10: Culture Clash*

## ~13~
# BABY'S GOT MOJO

"Jayd, where have you been?" Chase says, intoxicated. "You missed most of the party, girl. That's the best part about college, shawty."

"Please don't call me that," I say, irritated. I know that he has no idea of what I just went through but I'm not in the mood to be light.

"What's wrong? Did something happen?" Chase says, noticing the sweat dripping from my forehead. I don't think I've ever run so fast for that long.

"Yeah, I'm okay. Just took a midnight stroll."

"You walked from the hotel to here? Why did you do that?" Chase asks, in disbelief. "Ivan would've taken you anywhere that you wanted to go?"

"Sometimes it feels good to walk, you feel me?" Not sprint like I just did, which has me short of breath. I need to work out more.

"Girl, let me get you a bottled water. I'll be right back." Chase disappears into the crowded room and leaves me posted up in the corner. The walls are lined with framed photos of the fraternity members as well as their sister sorority. I can't imagine Chase pledging any fraternity, especially not a black one. Something tells me he's not one to blindly follow orders.

"Excuse me, miss. You have an uncanny resemblance to someone I used to know," the older gentleman says, staring a little too hard.

"Oh, I'm sure you don't know me. I'm just visiting with a friend." Where's Chase with my water? A sistah is more than parched.

"Where are your people from originally?" he asks, continuing the inquisition. Why is he so curious about me? What's he even doing here in the first place? Chase told me that his grandfather stopped by earlier to officially introduce him to the other members and then left. This is a young people's party, and this dude is anything but.

"Right here, actually." Something tells me not to reveal my identity. There's something a bit too eerie about him for my taste.

"Is that right?" he asks, moving closer to me. I'm becoming a bit uncomfortable with his approach. What is it with this dude?

"I used to know a lady, lovely woman really, with eyes very similar to yours except they were the brightest green that I've ever seen," he says, probing my eyes for recognition of my lineage. "Her name was Lynn Mae. She came from a line of women with green eyes, even passed them on to one of her daughters, or so I heard. She left before I could lay eyes on the baby."

"Interesting," I say, standing up straight. I need to be ready to run again just in case Esmeralda sent this dude.

"Isn't it?" he says. His eyes drift down to the jade bracelets on my left wrist. "Family traits are hard to hide, my dear. Blood always tells the truth."

I spot Chase heading my way with the cold drink. "Jayd, they're playing spades in the back," he says, unknowingly blowing my cover. "Want to join?"

"Jayd, as in Queen Jayd? I knew it," the elder says, staring at me as if he's seen a ghost. "Mon Dieu." He bows at me feet and touches the ground three times in acknowledgement of my lineage's crown.

Oh hell. I'm in no mood for this.

"Get up. Get up!" I say, impatiently. The other guests are too distracted by the loud music and free flowing alcohol to be concerned with our scene.

"Can I help you, bruh?" Chase asks, handing me the bottle. "Did you lose something?"

"Yes, I did. We all did. But I have a feeling that I've found her."

*"Jayd, you need to bless this man by touching each of his shoulders and giving him permission to rise. Otherwise he's going to feel that you've cursed him,"* Maman says, instructing me to perform the act that Mama does when people bow to her. Rather than argue, I follow instructions.

The man rises with a smile and thanks me in French.

"Jayd, I think it's time to turn it in," Chase says, protectively wrapping his arm across my shoulders. "Have a good night, man."

"You as well. Protect the young queen," he says, still smiling. "She's a rarity." He lifts my hands to his lips and kisses my knuckles. "We need her and her blessings always."

"Will do," Chase says, leading me away from the uncomfortable encounter. "What the hell was that about?" he asks once we step outside.

190

"I have no idea. He never even introduced himself."

Ivan opens the truck door for us to step inside. It doesn't feel like it's after one in the morning but the clock doesn't lie. It's been such a long day. I'm looking forward to getting back in the comfortable king-sized bed in our suite.

"You just have that affect on people." Chase nudges my shoulder with his. "You hungry?"

To tell the truth I could eat a little something. "Sure. What did you have in mind?"

"It's never to late or early for beignets. Ivan, would you mind heading to du Monde?"

"Sure thing, Mr. Carmichael."

"I already had one but you're right. That sounds delicious."

When we pull up to the café the line is wrapped around the outdoor patio, and the parking is even worse.

"I'm going to park on the other side of Jackson Square near the cathedral."

Both Chase and I are too tired to move. Ivan offers to stand in line for us and we gladly accept.

"It's nice having a driver, isn't it?" Chase says, touching the back of my hand with his knee.

"Yes. Very. It's also nice having a rich friend who let's you roll with him."

"Girl, you know it ain't nothing but a chicken wing. I'm glad you could come and enjoy yourself, weird old dudes bowing at your feet aside."

"Me too." Chase's scent is intoxicating in the close space. I can't help but miss his lips, his arms, and his touch.

*"Then kiss him already,"* Maman says. *"He'll remember everything for as long as you want him to until you stop kissing."*

*"How's that possible?"* And why didn't I know about this sooner?

*"It's called mojo, baby. You're not the first one of us who's had to erase a lover's memories in order to protect him. Try it. You can thank me later."*

Chase leans back in the leather seat and closes his eyes. This is the perfect opportunity to test Maman's suggestion.

192

"Jayd, what are you doing?" Chase asks as I open his arms and place them by his side.

Ignoring his question, I climb onto his lap and kiss him. I can feel the surge of energy return to his body. He closes his arms around my waist and returns my affection tenfold.

"I've missed you so much," I say, between nibbles.

"I didn't go anywhere, baby," he says, rubbing my back. He moves his lips down to my neck and kisses one of my favorite spots. "Can you reach in my back pocket and unwrap a condom?"

"What are you talking about? We're in a truck, and Ivan will be back soon with our pastries."

"We're on a relatively quiet street, and no one can see through these windows. Besides, he's going to be in line for a while and I can't wait until we get back to the hotel. But if you're not comfortable I can stop."

"No, don't stop kissing me," I say, remembering Maman's words. It's about time I stepped out of my comfort zone. And he's right. We have time and opportunity. "I don't want to wait, either."

We make love in front of the Catholic Church where Maman got married. Our reunion couldn't be more blessed. Too bad he won't remember it soon after, but I'll take what I can get. It is indeed the perfect trip. Too bad it has to end.


Our plane landed a couple of hours ago at LAX and I already miss New Orleans. Yesterday we spent the day shopping and eating after his school meetings. I stopped by a few voodoo supply places and stocked up with items that aren't so readily available locally. Chase even got out of the truck and held the bags for me while Ivan waited patiently. Chase doesn't understand much about what it is that I do but he's always supportive.

Instead of going back to my mom's place I decided to come back to my grandparent's house. I've been camped out in the spirit room ever since looking for something to help Mama snap back into the real world. I need to get gangsta with my shit and dare I say follow Esmeralda's advice. If I have to get dark and cold with my powers to defeat Rousseau, then so be it. I tried it Mama's way, but it's not working and she's no help as long as she's love drunk.

So far the spirit book has no suggestions on helping my

grandmother help us. We've probably never had a situation like this before. If we did it wasn't recorded.

"What's this?" I say aloud. Lexi's ears perk up without her head moving. She's always good company. "There's an incantation for going rogue. Apparently it's a spell that I cast on myself to make me not give a shit in order to accomplish a difficult task." I look at my reflection in the mirror and smile. "Sounds just like what the doctor ordered."

*"Or the godmother."* Esmeralda sounds different. I'm not sure what it is, but there's something about her voice that doesn't sit well with me.

"You're not my godmother, Esmeralda," I say, aloud. "Get over it."

Lexi growl's at the mention of our dead neighbor's name. Maybe I should keep this conversation to myself.

*"Maybe not officially, but we both know that I'm the only one who can really help you with this issue."*

The more her voice speaks into my head the more difficult it becomes to look away from my reflection. I recall Maman's warning about being trapped in Esmeralda's vision. After all of the research that I've done, it seems that Esmeralda's way is the fastest and most surefire plan to deal with Rousseau. If I can control her sight like Maman

195

suggested, then I can also control her without her realizing I'm on to her scheme.

*"What makes you think that you can help me from the grave?"*

*"I brought your grandmother out of her voodoo shell to be one of the baddest queens in recent history, as you saw from that man's reaction to you as her granddaughter,"* Esmeralda says, hissing. *"Only when she decided to get gangster with her sight did she reign the way she was born to do. But then she married your grandfather, had kids, and became domesticated."*

*"Sounds like you're hating to me,"* I think, simultaneously checking out my glow in the mirror. I have to admit, New Orleans also left me with a different swag, or maybe it was being back with Chase that helped. I've never felt more invigorated.

*"Yes, I admit that I was jealous of her life, but not for the sake of wanting it. I was no longer the best friend of the most powerful queen because she surrendered her power for love. Don't make that mistake, Jayd. Let others live mundane lives. You, child, are meant to shine, even in the dark. Don't be afraid to do just that."*

Again, she's making a lot of sense this evening. *"Okay. I'll cast the spell."*

*"Trust me, Jayd. Going rogue is the only way to beat him. He's gone*

196

*completely off the radar and that's always a dangerous thing. Why do you think I've always kept him on such a tight leash? I know my pet well, and he's at his best tamed. Otherwise, he's a lost soul."*

I mentally read the spell several times over, too afraid to give it verbal power. Once it's cast there's no turning back. The spell has to play itself out completely with no time constraint.

*"What's taking so long? Say the words so we can get on with this!"* Esmeralda commands.

*"I'm not sure if this is the right solution for our problem. What if I go too dark?"*

*"Everyone's got a dark side, Jayd, including your precious grandmother and you. We all need the balance of both to thrive in this world. Cast the spell and watch the magic happen."*

I take a deep breath and give power to the spell, repeating it three times as the book instructs.

"Excellent," Esmeralda says, unusually mellow. "It is done."

She leaves me alone to contemplate what I've just done. I'm not sure what not giving a shit feels like because I'm also concerned with other people's problems. If everything goes according to plan, that should no longer be an issue. Coupled with Maman's request to Legba to remove obstacles, trapping Rousseau should go as smoothly as trapping a rabid animal can. No one ever said rocking my crown would be easy.

~14~
## LA CORONACION

"Did you know that it is true: If you die in your dreams you die in real life? And so it is in reverse. If you don't die in your dreams, you don't die at all. You remain in limbo until such time," Maman says, appearing on the bed next to mine where her daughter sleeps. "Welcome to my world, Jayd, where I exist between everywhere and nowhere. In here, I'm the one and only queen. But out there, that queen is you."

She reaches across the small nightstand that separates the twin beds. Our space transforms from the small bedroom into the stunning historical cathedral she was married in.

"It is time," Maman says, walking me down the aisle of the massive church. When we reach the altar several of our ancestors appear, including Queen Califia.

"Please bow your head, Mademoiselle," the same man who incessantly questioned me at the frat party says. One side of his face is painted red and the other black.

"Listen to your Legba, Jayd. He will always lead you in the right *direction."*

*"Oui, Maman." When did I learn how to speak French?*

*Our ancestors each take turns saying blessings over the gold crown suspended above my head. Maman has the last word, claims the crown from Legba, and places it on my head. The metal feels cool against my skin and is heavier than it looks.*

*"There will always be enemies to contend with and battles to be won," Queen Califia says, kissing my forehead. "Remember that the biggest fights are in your own head."*

*"Now that you've got that crown, wear it and wear it proud," Maman says, following suit. "It's yours to do with what you will, Queen Jayd. Use it wisely and wield its power responsibly. And, whatever you do, don't ever give away your ashe."*

*"And you can start by locking Rousseau up immediately. You have all of the tools that you need to make it happen." Queen Califia pulls a leash out of her side holster with a spiked collar attached.*

*"You have to go dark and get gutter to trap him," Maman says, passing me a leather whip. "He won't be expecting that. It's the only way to control him. He won't respect you as his master any other way."*

*What the hell? This is all over my head. "I don't want to control him or be his master."*

*"You have to, Jayd. You have no choice in the matter." Queen Califia stands next to Legba who's in full agreement with them both.*

*"Your grandmother's powers would be the best to use in this situation," Maman says, removing the wooden rosary from around her neck and placing it over my head. "Trust me, Jayd. A mother knows her daughter's full capability, even if she doesn't want to acknowledge it. Your grandmother's fear was going too dark for fear of losing her husband, and I can't fault her for that. All she ever wanted was the family that she didn't have as a child. Because of that desire, love became her limitation."*

*"Don't we all have our limits?" I feel overwhelmed by my new status. Whoever said being a queen was fun never had to wear her crown.*

*"Yes, of course, my dear. And we also move past our limitations and own that shit."*

*"Hurry, Jayd. It's time to face your fears and trap Rousseau," Maman says, helping me to my feet. "He must be leashed and tamed. Only balanced beings can run wild, and he is certainly not that."*

*"Agreed." Queen Califia nods in recognition.*

*"Your grandmother's asleep now. Find her dreams and snatch her sight. Don't worry. As long as she doesn't resist everything will be fine."*

*"I don't see Mama giving up her sight willingly. What happens then?"*

*"Don't worry about that, or have you forgotten the spell that you just cast? Keep your eyes focused on the endgame. Everything that happens up until that point is not your concern."*

*Maman's right, as usual. I focus my energy on sifting through the various dreams I'm privy to until I find my grandmother's.*

*She's in the spirit room baking a lemon pound cake, my grandfather's favorite dessert.*

*"Jayd, what are you doing here?" she asks, gleefully cleaning up the flour and other ingredients spread out on the kitchen counter. "Daddy should be home soon and there's so much left to do before he arrives."*

*"I know, Mama. There's always work to do."*

*"Something tells me this isn't a casual visit," she says, removing her apron.*

*"Mama, I need to borrow your sight." I walk to the other side of the tall island and face her head on.*

*"The hell you do," she says, tossing the apron onto the countertop. She places her hands on her hips ready for whatever comes next.*

"Mama, I'm sorry. You leave me no choice." *Unfortunately for her, I have our ancestors and Legba on my side.*

*"You and I both know that's a load of crap, girl. You always have a choice. You're just making the wrong one and don't realize it yet. You'll*

learn soon enough if you try to cross me," she says, pointing her manicured index finger at me. "Best believe it won't end well for you."

"Mama, it's not a competition. It's an evolution." I lock onto my grandmother's green eyes and force her to look me straight in my brown eyes. "This isn't a battle between the two of us. It's for the good of our lineage."

"You don't know what's good for our lineage, little girl. You're a child!"

Mama attempts to block me from controlling her sight. What she doesn't realize is that I'm sleepwalking through her dream, and therefor she has no control over this reality. The dream world is my world, and I will rock this shit.

"I'm not a child anymore, Mama. I love you, but this time you're wrong. Please, surrender to the process and let me do my job."

"Surrender? To you, my child's child? That'll never happen. Over my dead body if it ever does."

"That's what I'm trying to avoid."

Mama's eyes glow with a red hue behind them. She's beyond pissed. "Now that you're no longer a virgin you think that you can challenge me in my own house? Little girl, please. I eat people like you for lunch."

"Not lately you don't. You're too busy catering to your husband to check anyone, including me."

"We'll see about that."

We circle one another, never letting go of each other's sight. Mama stops in front of me, her jade eyes aglow with all of the power she can throw at me. I accept it all and absorb her sight.

"What are you doing?" Mama asks, realizing that I'm in control of this situation.

"Taking care of our business like you taught me to." Her sight, unlike my mom's and Esmeralda's, is hot. The heat in my head catches me off guard and causes me to shut my eyes to keep from screaming out in pain.

"That's right. I'm the teacher and you're the student. You can't handle my powers. Stop playing with things you don't understand."

"Oh, I understand your powers more than you know. Thanks to our ancestors I also understand mine better." The heat in my head diminishes and spreads throughout the rest of my body. I open my eyes and feel their green shimmer. Mama's sight feels unique to the others that I've snatched before.

"That's enough fooling around, Jayd. Give me back my sight before I take it from you."

"You know that's not how this works, Mama," I say, sympathetic for her loss. "I have to go and handle the house next door. Don't worry, I'll return your sight to you when I'm done."

"Jayd, don't you walk out of that door," Mama says, completely helpless to stop me. She looks around the spirit room and realizes that she's not going to win this battle. "Jayd!"

Mama runs after me and pulls my arm. She forces me to again look her in the eye but this time it's to her detriment.

"Mama, I'm sorry but you're not leaving me much of a choice."

She slaps me across the face again. My face stings from the impact.

"You always have a choice." Mama grabs me by the shoulder and attempts to shake me, but my growing powers won't allow her to hurt me any more.

My eyes take on a life of their own, crippling my grandmother like the enemy that she's not.

*"You can't use my own powers against me!"* Mama falls to the floor, *crying from the impact of her sight. "It's not right."*

*"Stay asleep, Mama. By the time you wake up in the morning everything will be back to normal, I promise. I love you."*

*I hate to see my grandmother in pain, but she brought this on herself. It's time for me to wake up and kick some supernatural ass.*

I shake myself awake and rush out of bed. I'll check on my grandmother later. Right now it's all about our neighbors and their diabolic menagerie. Without hesitation, I switch my focus from Mama's dreams to next door.

"Queen Jayd. How lovely to see you again, but not really," Rousseau says, puffing on a cigar. At least he's in his human form for the moment. He looks stronger than he's been since Esmeralda crossed over.

"This can be easy or difficult, Rousseau. You choose." I notice Misty seated at the kitchen table counting coins. There are dozens of squawking animals in the kitchen emaciated from hunger.

"I choose neither, mon amour. I hear congratulations are in order to the new reine. How lovely for you, little queen." He laughs loudly and reveals his sharpened canines. "Too bad your crown can't save you tonight."

"Bye, bitch," Misty says, snarling in my direction. "It's time you paid for your sins on our house."

Misty morphs into the snake I've seen her as before and rapidly slithers toward us through the opened back door. Rousseau simultaneously changes shape into the bat that I saw Misty feed the other night. He flies over my head while Misty attacks my feet.

"As above, so shall it be below," Maman says. Use all of your powers, Jayd. You have three sights at your disposal, with your grandmother's being the most pivotal. Take care of business!"

Rather than fear the animals I focus on controlling them. I take out the whip first and wield it as a warning. Both creatures back up at the crack of the tool, shocked at its presence.

"Submit willing or not. Either way, you belong to me." I crack the whip once more and Misty retreats back inside. Rousseau, on the other hand, decides to test my patience.

"You think you can catch me, young one? Let's see if you think you're as bad as those wretched women in your lineage have set you up to believe." Rousseau flies outside of the screen door and soars high above the house. After an impressive sky routine, he dives toward me and I'm ready for his attack.

"Gotcha!" I scream, whipping Queen Califia's leash and collar around his neck. The more he struggles the tighter the grip.

"You wretched shrew!" Rousseau yells, but it's no use. He's mine now and he knows it.

"Call me whatever you like. As long as you realize who's ultimately in control, it's truly inconsequential to me."

"You do realize that this is all temporary, little girl. I always escape one way or another."

"If you say so. But in the meantime, you're going to submit to me and do as I say. Is that understood?"

Rousseau returns to his true canine state, his eyes sullen as he accepts his stature.

"Yes, my queen. I am here to serve you and only you."

"Excellent," I say, tying the leash to the banister. "I'm so glad that we finally understand each other. And please let your other housemates know that there's a new queen in town, and she takes no shit. See you in the morning."

## EPILOGUE

When I wake up I know that I will feel different, and that's fine with me. I used to fight my powers. But now I just don't care one way or the other what anyone thinks of me, including the people that I love. My mission is clear and I choose to honor my gifts, come hell or high water. Whether or not Mama will ever forgive me for snatching her sight through her dreams I don't know, but I can't worry about that. In time I'm sure she'll understand. And hopefully she'll accept that she has been dethroned earlier than anticipated.

# Discussion Questions

1. Was Jayd right to turn her back on Mickey in her time of need? How would you handle a similar situation?

2. Do think that Mama is in her right state of mind for choosing her relationship over everything else? Would you do the same thing?

3. In what way do you think that Jayd and Chase can maintain a relationship, if at all?

4. Have you ever been to New Orleans? Are there other places that you would like to travel to? Name a few and why you'd like to visit.

5. Does everyone have a dark side? If so, should she/he honor that side? Why or why not?

6. Is Nickey in a better place even if she's not with her mother? Explain your answer.

7. Do think that Jayd betrayed any of her friends with her actions? Explain.

8. Is it ever okay to choose your own happiness over someone else's, even if it's someone that you love and/or like? Please give an example.

9. If Netta had the power to fire Mama do you think that she should do so? Share an example of a time when you've been disappointed by a best friend, if relevant.

10. Have you ever been afraid of change? Give an example of a time when you were forced to change and how it affected your life.

Stay tuned for the next book
in the DRAMA HIGH series,
NO LIMIT

## RECOMMENDED READING

Listed below are a few of my favorite writers. The list is in no particular order and always changing. Please feel free to send me your favorites at **www.DramaHigh.com.**

OCTAVIA E. BUTLER

ALICE WALKER

ZORA NEALE HURSTON

TINA MCELROY ANSA

JAMES BALDWIN

MARYSE CONDE

MADISON SMART BELL

RHONDA BYRNE

NAPOLEON HILL

JACKIE COLLINS

MARY HIGGINS CLARK

J.K. ROWLING

STEPHEN KING

IYANLA VANZANT

R.M. JOHNSON

AMY TAN

NATHAN MCCALL

NIKKI GIOVANNI

EDWIDGE DANTICAT

J. CALIFORNIA COOPER

TONI CADE BAMBARA

RICHARD WRIGHT

GLORIA NAYLOR

JAMES PATTERSON

LUISAH TEISH

QUEEN AFUA

BRI. MAYA TIWARI

HILL HARPER

JOSEPH CAMPBELL

TANANARIVE DUE

ANNE RICE

L.A. BANKS

FRANCINE PASCAL

SANDRA CISNEROS

DANIELLE STEELE

CAROLYN RODGERS

CHIEF FAMA

GWENDOLYN BROOKS

BELL HOOKS

AMIRI BARAKA

CRISTINA GARCÍA

START YOUR OWN BOOK CLUB


Courtesy of the DRAMA HIGH series


ABOUT THIS GUIDE

The following is intended to help you get the Book Club you've always wanted up and running!  Enjoy!

# Start Your Own Book Club

A Book Club is not only a great way to make friends, but is also a fun and safe environment for you to express your views and opinions on everything from fashion to teen pregnancy? A Teen Book Club can also become a forum or venue to air grievances and plan remedies for problems.

## The People
To start, all you need is yourself and at least one other person. There's no criteria for who this person or persons should be other than a desire to read and a commitment to read and discuss during a certain time frame.

## The Rules
Just like in Jayd's life, sometimes even Book Club discussions can be filled with much drama. People tend to disagree with each other, cut each other off when speaking, and take criticism personally. So, there should be some ground rules:

1. Do not attack people for their ideas or opinions.
2. When you disagree with a book club member on a point, disagree respectfully. This means that you do not denigrate another person for their ideas or even their ideas, themselves i.e. no name calling or saying, "That's stupid!" Instead, say, "I can respect your position, however, I feel differently."
3. Back up your opinions with concrete evidence, either from the book in question or life in general.
4. Allow every one a turn to comment.
5. Do not cut a member off when they are speaking. Respectfully, wait your turn.
6. Critique only the idea (and do so responsibly; again, saying simply, "That's stupid!" is not allowed). Do not critique the person.
7. Every member must agree to and abide by the ground rules.

*Feel free to add any other ground rules you think might be necessary.

### The Meeting Place

Once you've decided on members, and agreed to the ground rules, you should decide on a place to meet. This could be the local library, the school library, your favorite restaurant, a bookstore, or a member's home. Remember, though, if you decide to hold your sessions at a member's home, the location should rotate to another member's home for the next sessions. It's also polite for guests to bring treats when attending a Book Club meeting at a member's home. If you choose to hold your meetings in a public place, always remember to ask the permission of the librarian or store manager. If you decide to hold your meetings in a local bookstore, ask the manager to post a flyer in the window announcing the Book Club to attract more members if you so desire.

### Timing is Everything

Teenagers of today are all much busier than teenagers of the past. You're probably thinking, "Between Chorus Rehearsals, the Drama Club, and oh yeah, my job, when will I ever have time to read another book that doesn't feature Romeo and Juliet!" Well, there's always time, if it's time well-planned and time planned ahead. You and your Book Club can decide to meet as often or as little as is appropriate for your bustling schedules. **Once a month** is a favorite option. **Sleepover Book Club** meetings—if you're open to excluding one gender—is also a favorite option. And in this day of high-tech, savvy teens, **Internet Discussion Groups** are also an appealing option. Just choose what's right for you!

Well, you've got the people, the ground rules, the place, and the time. All you need now is a book!

### The Book

Choosing a book is the most fun. ROGUE is of course an excellent choice, and since it's a series, you won't soon run out of books to read and discuss. Your Book Club can also have comparative discussions as you compare the first book, THE FIGHT, to the second, SECOND CHANCE, and so on.

But depending on your reading appetite, you may want to veer outside of the DRAMA HIGH series. That's okay. There are plenty of options available.

Don't be afraid to mix it up. Nonfiction is just as good as fiction, and a fun way to learn about from whence we came without the monotony of a history book. Science Fiction and Fantasy can be fun too!

And always, always, research the author. You may find the author has a website where you can post your Book Club's questions or comments. The author may even have an email address available so you can correspond directly. Authors will also sit in on your Book Club, either in person, or on the phone, and this can be a fun way to discuss the boo as well!

**The Discussion**
Every good Book Club discussion starts with questions. **ROGUE,** as well as every other book in the **DRAMA HIGH** series comes along with a Reading Group Guide for your convenience, though of course, it's fine to make up your own. Here are some sample questions to get started:

1. What's this book all about anyway?
2. Who are the characters? Do we like them? Do they remind us of real people?
3. Was the story interesting? Were real issues of concern to you examined?
4. Were there details that didn't quite work for you or ring true?
5. Did the author create a believable environment—one that you can visualize?
6. Was the ending satisfying?
7. Would you read another book from this author?

**Record Keeper**
It's generally a good idea to have someone keep track of the books you read. Often libraries and schools will hold reading drives where you're rewarded for having read a certain number of books in a certain time period. Perhaps, a pizza party awaits!

**Get Your Teachers and Parents Involved**

Teachers and Parents love it when kids get together and read. So involve your teachers and parents. Your Book Club may read a particular book where it would help to have an adult's perspective as part of the discussion. Teachers may also be able to include what you're doing as a Book Club in the classroom curriculum. That way books you love to read like DRAMA HIGH can find a place in your classroom alongside of the books you don't love to read so much.

# KEEPING THE SECRET

### A Novel

## RM JOHNSON

1

I sat in the crowded mall food court with my girlfriend, Lauren. She was beautiful with her long brown hair, light brown skin, full lips and almond shaped eyes.

We were in love. We knew that after only dating for three months and had been inseparable since.

Lauren dipped one of her fries in some ketchup then held it out for me. I snapped it from her fingers like a dog snatching table scraps.

"Next time get my fingers while you're at it, Ebban," Lauren joked.

I smiled, munching on the fry. I took a sip of my orange pop then felt my cell vibrating in my pocket. I fished it out and took a look at the text message. It read—

I SEE U.

I quickly scanned the crammed food court. Adults walked around wearing shorts, T-shirts and flip-flops, holding the hands of their children. Teens wearing sagging jeans and backward baseball caps carried trays to their tables and stood in small groups taking sips from their pop cups.

I was looking but I didn't see anyone. At least no one I knew.

"What's wrong?" Lauren asked.

"Uh...nothing." I smiled.

"Who was that who called you?"

"It was a text."

"Who texted you?"

"Oh. Matt," I lied. Matt was my best friend. He played forward on our high school basketball team. He was tall and good looking.

"What did he want?" Lauren asked.

I was about to answer her when the phone vibrated again in my hand. I glanced back at the screen.

U 2 LOOK LIKE UR HAVING FUN. U LOOK LIKE A REGULAR COUPLE.

HOW NICE.


I tried to hide my anger as I answered Lauren's question. "Matt asked if I wanna shoot ball later today. Now he's texting me back saying if I'm scared he'll understand. I gotta let him know I'd whoop him with my eyes closed."

I punched several of the tiny keys with my thumbs.

223

# WHO IS THIS?!?

"Tell Matt I said hi," Lauren said.

"I will," I said, my heart beating hard as I looked up scanning the food court again. I was expecting to see someone off in a corner somewhere punching keys like I had just done. I saw no one.

My screen lit with the incoming text.

I THINK U KNO. MEET ME IN THE LITTLE BOY'S ROOM.

I pulled my eyes up from the tiny phone screen and shot a stare in the direction of the restroom. Men walked in, others walked out— nothing out of the ordinary.

NO!

I pushed my phone back into my jeans pocket, then picked up my cheeseburger and tore a bite out of it.

"Everything all right?"

I smiled, swallowed the food in my mouth, then leaned over the table, puckering. "Everything is perfect, babe."

Lauren leaned over, met me halfway and pecked me on the lips.

My phone went off again. I thought of ignoring it, thought better, and pulled it out. "Sorry, babe," I said, eyeing the message.

U DON'T COME 2 ME, I'LL COME 2 U. ☺

I nervously grabbed another fry, popped it in my mouth as though there was nothing wrong. "Gotta go to the bathroom. Be right back," I told Lauren.

"Okay," she said, looking concerned.

Stepping into the men's room, I looked around cautiously like I was being set up, like I was about to be jumped. Before me were six urinals, sinks, and five stalls. One of the doors was closed.

I stepped in front of it, cleared my throat as loud as I could.

Something moved behind the door. I bent over to see a pair of sneakers. I heard the latch being undone. The door swung open.

"Come in," the boy behind the door said, smiling.

I looked over my shoulder to see that no one had entered after me then stepped into the narrow stall space.

225

The boy who stood in front of me was named Colin. He was thin, 5'9"—two inches shorter than me. He had medium brown skin, a narrow, pointy nose, and wore wire framed glasses.

"What do you want, Colin?" I said, irritated.

"You can't keep it a secret for the rest of your life. People are gonna find out."

"Find out what?" I said, daring him to say what I knew was on his mind.

"That you're—"

"I'm what?" I took another step closer, my eyes narrowed and fists clinched.

Colin's chest heaved. I saw fear in his eyes. "You can't hide forever. No one can," Colin said, his voice quivering. "It'll get out."

"There's nothing *to* get out," I said, beginning to worry that he had told someone about the times he and I met in the park and talked.

"We had this conversation and you said—"

I grabbed him tight by the arm. "You telling people something?" My voice was a harsh.

Colin swallowed the lump in his throat. "No."

"You keep it that way, because there's nothing to tell, right?"

He stared wide-eyed at me.

"Say it." I clamped down tighter on his arm. I didn't mean to hurt him, but he needed to know I was serious.

He winced. "There's...there's nothing to tell."

I stared at Colin a long moment, wishing I had never sought him out, that I never started this. I released him. I pushed open the stall door, about to step out, when Colin called me. I turned.

"Ebban, I won't say anything." He rubbed his wrist as though in serious pain. "But that doesn't mean people won't find out. Trust me, they always find out."

I walked out of the men's room, frowning.

Outside, Lauren was waiting, holding two ice cream cones. I forced a smile. I kissed her on the lips. "You bought one for me?"

"I know vanilla is your favorite," she said, handing me the cone.

"My favorite, only after you," I said, wrapping my arm around her and leading her toward the mall's exit. I looked over my shoulder hoping I would never see Colin again.

## 2

Sebastian Akers stood on the curb, looking up at a huge, beautiful, brown brick home.

The people who lived in this house had money, Sebastian told himself. They had to to live here, out in the expensive suburb Sebastian had to take two busses and a train to get to.

Standing on the curb like that, the bright, late afternoon Sunday sun beating down on his very light skin—he felt inadequate. He wore his typical attire, black denim straight leg jeans, black Converse All-star low tops and a polo shirt, the collar up. His kinky-curly, dirty blonde hair was cut into a semi-Mohawk, product freezing the strands on the top of his head.

Sebastian looked down at the scrap of paper he had written an address on. 867 Dunway Road. He looked up again at the house. This was the place.

He spoke to the owner yesterday evening while locked in his bedroom, his laptop open, a search engine glowing on the screen before him. A White Pages phone book sat by his hip, opened to the A's.

"Is this Mr. Phillip Akers?"

"Yes."

"I'm sorry to interrupt you, sir, but my name is Sebastian Akers. I know this will sound strange, but…" Sebastian's throat felt tight. He turned his head, glanced at his bedroom door as if worried that his foster mother was just behind it, waiting to hear him fail so she could laugh in his face.

"Hello," the man on the phone said, bringing Sebastian's attention back to the call.

"Yes. I'm sorry. The reason I'm calling is to ask you if you have any children."

There was a long pause on the other end before Mr. Akers said in a polite tone, "I don't know what business of yours that is."

"I was given up for adoption when I was two years old, Mr. Akers. I tried to locate my mother but found out that she died eight years ago. Now I'm calling—"

"Hold it," Mr. Akers said. "You're not calling to ask if I'm your father are you?"

Sebastian hesitated. "Uh…yes."

229

"Sorry," Mr. Akers said, chuckling some again. "I'm not. But good luck in finding him." He hung up the phone.

Sebastian tried calling the man back three times last night, but he suspected Mr. Akers was screening the phone numbers and wouldn't pick up again.

That was what led Sebastian out here to the man's house. It took a little investigating, but he was able to come up with his home address. Sebastian knew how to research. It was required of every journalist, and that's what Sebastian was—editor of the school's newspaper. One day he told himself he would be a Pulitzer Prize winning journalist/entertainment reporter.

Now, walking up the path to the house, standing on the huge front porch, Sebastian wondered if he should've come here. But he needed proof. There weren't many Akers in the phone book, which he was grateful for. But of the number of them that were, he needed definite verification that none of them were his father.

If Mr. Akers just would've picked up the phone, given Sebastian the information he was looking for, he wouldn't have had to confront the man like this.

Sebastian rang the doorbell and nervously waited for someone to answer.

He waited for almost a full minute, turning his back on the door, thinking about just leaving. He heard his foster mother's hateful voice echo in his head. "Why would you do that to yourself?" She said two months ago when Sebastian told her he was going to try to find his father.

"What if he's looking for me, too?"

Sebastian's foster mother—who he never called Ma or Mommy or even Mother, but Ms. Peel—grinned, then appeared as though she was about to burst out laughing.

"If he was looking for you, what makes you think after seeing you he'd want you? Your mother gave you away and your father left before that for a reason. You showing up now would only let him know he was right in taking off."

After that comment, Sebastian turned, walked through the deteriorating old house to his tiny bed room, closed the door then lowered himself in bed to go to sleep.

Now, still on Mr. Akers' porch, he felt like walking away even more. Sebastian couldn't do it. He had to find out if this man was actually his father.

He turned around to see a man standing behind the glass of the front door. He was tall and much older than Sebastian would've guessed.

Mr. Akers, who Sebastian could fully see now, looked to be in his late sixties, with his gray hair and full gray beard. The man smiled, opened the door and said, "You're the boy who called yesterday, aren't you?"

"Yes, sir," Sebastian said.

"I'm sorry I didn't answer your calls again, but—"

"No need to apologize, sir," Sebastian said. This man obviously wasn't his father. He was too old and he looked nothing like the man on the one old dog eared snapshot Sebastian had.

Sebastian had been told his father was 20 years old when Sebastian was born. That would've made his father 36 now. Sebastian sadly accepted this wasn't the man. "Do you happen to have any sons, sir?" Sebastian asked with fading hope.

"I'm sorry," Mr. Akers said. "I have three daughters."

Sebastian lowered his head. "I'm sorry to have bothered you like this." He didn't move from where he stood, just remained looking down at his shoes.

"You must really want to find him," Sebastian heard the old man say.

"I do."

After another short pause, Mr. Akers said, "If there's anything I can do to help."

It sounded like pity to Sebastian. He hated pity.

"No. I'm fine," Sebastian said, not looking up. "Goodbye." He turned, and walked away.

## 3

Lauren and I were riding in my father's Infiniti truck, but Dad didn't tell us where we were going.

Lauren was supposed to have dropped me off at home after we came from the mall, but my father stepped out the front door, and said, "You two come in for a minute."

After walking in the house, my father said, "You weren't going home already, were you Lauren?"

My father was a good looking, square jawed man. He stayed clean shaven, got a hair cut every week, and on certain days he looked like he could pass for my older brother. All the girls at my school thought he was cute.

Dad was crazy about Lauren. Whenever he and I were alone, he would tell me about a girlfriend he had when he was my age that looked just like her.

One day we were watching basketball like we often do together. He took a sip from his bottle of soda, and I felt him just staring at the side of my face. I turned, looked back weirdly at him, smiling a little, and said, "What?"

"So...have you...you know..."

"You know what, Dad?"

"You know...had sex yet?"

I took a swallow from my bottle of chocolate milk, stalling. "Is there a time limit?"

"No," he chuckled, backing off some. "I'm just saying. It's okay if you want to. I mean, you'll be seventeen soon, and... "

"We just haven't discussed it yet, okay," I lied. Actually, we had discussed it several times, almost too many times. We were both virgins, but it was always Lauren telling me that she wanted me, that we were in love and we should express it physically.

It's not that I didn't want to. It's not that I didn't love her. I just wasn't sure if I could please her, or if I wanted her like that just yet.

Yes, there were times when we'd kiss, when we'd pet, and I'd feel excitement building and then when I thought of taking things a step further, I'd lose whatever motivation I had. I was scared that when it was time, I wouldn't be able to perform. I knew it might have been because of these thoughts I've been having lately, thoughts I would never want Lauren or anyone for that matter to ever find out about.

Dad pulled the truck into the parking lot of a BMW dealership.

"Okay, we're here."

Looking out the window at all the shiny, brand new cars, I said, "*Why* are we here?"

Dad turned to me smiling then stepped out the truck and closed the door without responding. I turned around to see if Lauren might have had a clue.

A huge smile was on her face. She reached over the back seat and started patting me excitedly on the shoulder. "You think he brought you here to...you think he's going to buy you—"

"No," I said, hoping that wasn't the reason we were here. I grabbed the door handle, pushed it open. "C'mon."

As Lauren and I walked hand in hand, Dad was already talking to a salesman, a short guy in khaki pants and a button down white shirt with the BMW logo on his left breast.

I knew what this was about and why my father was doing it. It was that "perfect son" stuff he was always talking and I was getting to the point where I just couldn't take it anymore.

If he only knew where I had just come from, had seen me in that bathroom stall threatening Colin. If he had known that I used to chat with him online, that I did meet him in the park, and we would sit and have conversations about his lifestyle.

"Dad," I said, standing beside him.

"How you doing, son?" the salesman said, giving me a rosy cheeked smile. "My name is Mr. Mathis." He extended his hand. I shook it then turned back to my father.

"Dad, can I talk to you?"

"Ebban," he said my name like I had no clue what was about to happen. "Mr. Mathis is about to show you a car I had him find especially for you."

"Dad, I really need to talk to you."

"Ebban, did you hear what I just said?"

"Yeah, Dad, but I really need—"

"Fine. Excuse us, please," Dad said to Lauren and the salesman.

We walked over and stood beside a sleek new, silver 3 series. "Why are we here?" I asked.

Dad chuckled. "Yeah, right. Like you don't know."

"If you're about to buy me a new car, I don't want it. I don't deserve it."

He laughed again. "It's not a new car, but it's a nice old one."

"Please, Dad. I still don't want it."

"Whose high school basketball team won all-city last year?"

"Ours, Dad."

"Who was the star player? Who made the winning shot at the buzzer? Who's the number one player in the city, being recruited by every major basketball school in the country, and even hearing rumors that some NBA teams would love if he considered skipping college altogether? Who is that kid?"

"Me, Dad," I said, annoyed.

"Oh yeah, and what's happening on Monday?"

"Okay, Dad, I get it."

"No, son. What's happening on Monday?"

"I'm getting an award for best all around student."

"Oh yeah, that's right. I almost forgot that. But you don't deserve this car that I'm about to buy you. A car that I had planned on buying you since the first day I brought you home from the hospital wrapped in blankets and had no idea you'd turn out to be the perfect son."

"Man, Dad, I'm not perfect!" I said much louder than I should've. I noticed that Lauren and Mr. Mathis glanced over in my direction. I turned back to my father. "I got faults like everybody else. And what if..."

"What if what, son?" Dad said.

I stood there staring at him, wanting so badly to just get this off of my chest. "I can't take the car, Dad," I said, sadly.

"I'm not asking you to take it. I don't need your permission to give you something I think you deserve."

"Dad, no," I said.

"Then tell me why. Tell me why I shouldn't buy this for you and I won't."

I looked up at Dad, but could not say a word.

"Good," Dad said, wrapping his arm around my shoulder and leading me back toward Lauren and the salesman. "We're about to get you a car.

CPSIA information can be obtained
at www.ICGtesting.com
Printed in the USA
LVOW04s2145070616
491656LV00014B/280/P